C000050908

NANCY WARREN

LUCK
OF THE IRIS

VILLAGE FLOWER SHOP
COZY MYSTERY - BOOK 4

Luck of the Iris, Village Flower Shop Book 4, Copyright © 2023 by Nancy Warren

Cover Design by Lou Harper of Cover Affairs

All rights reserved.

No part of this book may be reproduced in any form or by any electronic or mechanical means, including information storage and retrieval systems, without written permission from the author, except for the use of brief quotations in a book review.

Thank you for respecting the author's work.

ISBN: ebook 978-1-990210-79-2

ISBN: print 978-1-990210-80-8

Ambleside Publishing

INTRODUCTION

Prettiest garden contest
How delightful...
How deadly

I thought judging the Willow Waters garden contest would be fun. A nice way to get to know a few more of my neighbors in this beautiful Cotswold village. I'd get to see how the best gardens grew, maybe nab a few tips for my own garden. I did not expect the competition to be to the death. Literally.

I'm Peony Bellefleur and I own Bewitching Blooms. I chose to be a florist for all the positive reasons you can imagine: people love flowers; they speak a language we all understand. Fresh blooms perk up an invalid, add celebration to a wedding, and welcome new babies (especially when I've added a bit of witch's magic to my bouquets). I agreed to judge the garden competition for the same reasons. Joy and happiness.

Well, that was a mistake.

Between missing persons, interfering gnomes, and a full moon celebration that goes wrong, it's been a busy time.

Come join me and my unusual friends in my latest adventure.

"A modern-day Agatha Christie. This mystery was as smooth as a Swiss watch and as cozy as a café au lait with a chocolate croissant." *****

And if you haven't met Rafe Crosyer yet, he's the gorgeous, sexy vampire in *The Vampire Knitting Club* series. You can get his origin story free when you join Nancy's no-spam newsletter at NancyWarrenAuthor.com.

Come join Nancy in her private Facebook group where we talk about books, knitting, pets, and life. www.facebook.com/groups/NancyWarrenKnitwits

LUCK OF THE IRIS

CHAPTER 1

I thought that judging the prettiest garden competition in a quiet village in the Cotswolds in England was about as low-pressure as a volunteer job could get. Boy, was I wrong.

I mean, when people say it's a contest to the death, they're usually talking about gladiators in a coliseum. At the very least, some serious wrestling action. But a gardening competition? Apart from deadheading, death's not the first thing which springs to mind.

But wait, I'm getting ahead of myself.

It was a particularly warm day in July. I know the villagers of Willow Waters (Willowers, as we called ourselves) were getting worried that it was too late in the season for a garden competition. As a proud flower shop owner, the truth was that I shared their concerns. However, nature was the greatest leveler: if it was a problem for one gardener, it was a problem for the rest. If one rosebush was overblown, the same was true for its neighbors.

In any case, the committee of Justine Johnson, the

village's new vicar; Arthur Higginsbottom, the president of our local historical society; Bernard Drake, the church organist; and me—the only person on the panel who actually had anything to do with flowers—had organized our first judges' meeting. Justine and I were both brand new to this kind of thing and, I think, shared the idea that it was going to be a fun, pleasant way to spend a few afternoons.

I mean, who wouldn't like to go and nose around your neighbors' gardens without feeling like a snoop?

We could stroll about to our heart's content, admire their patch of blooming sweet peas or their flowering herb garden or whatever it was that they were so proud of, and then we'd reconvene to pick a winner together. Simple, right?

But what I hadn't banked on was how the competition captured the imagination of the *whole* village—not just those participating. The annual competition was the brainchild of the town council, devised as a way to encourage the green thumbs to keep up the good work, and perhaps to inspire those who weren't putting quite so much effort into their gardens to pick up the spade, as it were. Because tourism is a very important industry in the Cotswolds, and the beautiful honey-colored stone cottages, the charming villages, and quaint shops are even more inspiring when surrounded by splendid blooms.

Not that there were many derelict patches of garden in our verdant village and its surrounding areas. Willowers tended to be very house-proud—or cottage-proud, as the case might be. There were those who'd been living here generation after generation and had inherited their lovely homes along with a strong sense of pride in their surroundings. With this group, it was like they didn't want to let down their forebears who'd gone to all the trouble of building their cottages stone by stone and planting the willows that gave our town its name.

And then there were the more recent transplants who wanted to fit in, a lot of them from London, or less frequently from overseas, like me—though I had the strange honor of being the only American in town.

There were also vacation rentals, and there were plenty of those. The savvy owners understood that their properties should look as postcard-pretty as possible so they could charge the big bucks to visitors who flocked to the Cotswolds seeking its quaint charm.

I guess all this is to say—everyone was invested in making Willow Waters the prettiest village in all of England. In my opinion, we succeeded.

However, as more than one social commentator has pointed out, behind every peaceful, beautiful English village is an opportunity for darkness to thrive. Open the chintz drapes and peek inside the living room, where a cozy fire crackles in the grate and a cat lies curled on the couch, and you may just discover a body lying on the floor. After almost three years in the village, I was starting to understand that Willow Waters was no different. We had our share of village joy, but with it came darkness, too. Death was no stranger to this corner of the Cotswolds.

So, as you can imagine, I found myself somewhat preoccupied that warm July day when my first customer of the morning entered Bewitching Blooms. The door was propped open with an upturned flower bucket in an attempt to let in a cool breeze, and if it hadn't been for Norman, my new lodger and fellow witch's parrot familiar, flapping around wildly, I might not even have noticed that I was no longer alone.

I looked up from my place at the workbench and smiled as a lady I'd never seen before bent down to admire a beautiful bunch of blue stocks.

Norman, guard-parrot objective completed, flew back to his favorite perch and promptly settled himself in for a nap. That bird sure did doze a lot in the warmer weather.

My new customer looked to be around sixty, with a wild mop of carrot-colored hair, and a few silver streaks at the temples. She was wearing a pair of green linen dungarees and a sleeveless cotton blouse.

I rose and greeted her with my usual offer of help, and the woman introduced herself as Colleen O'Brien. Her voice rolled with a soft Irish lilt.

"I've never been in before," she said, "and I must say I'm impressed with your selection. That love-in-a-mist is especially pretty. A humble cottage flower which gives any arrangement an airy feel."

I thanked her, genuinely touched by the compliment. Not that I blamed them, of course, but most customers were only concerned with their impending purchase and didn't take the time to notice how thoughtfully I'd chosen my blooms and arranged them. Not to mention the carefully curated array of extra gifts and cards, which could add quite a bit to a flower order. I wondered if Colleen was also in the floristry business and asked the newcomer if that was the case.

She shook her head. "I don't have my own shop, or sell flowers, but I am passionate about flowers in my own way. I grow them and like nothing more than to fill my home with cuttings from the garden. I do love to bring the beauty of my garden inside the house." She paused for a moment and took another look around the shop. "I see you have some fine red carnations. Of course, they must have come from Spain at this time of the year. I do so prefer locally-grown flowers."

I forced a pleasant smile. Not that I didn't agree with my new customer, but of course not everything I sold could be grown locally. If I was going to offer a fair variety of blooms, there was no choice but to buy imports. "I do try to keep my stock as local as possible. Same with the gift shop. All our candles are hand poured by a maker in the neighboring village. The incense is made by my mom," I added proudly.

This last detail seemed to impress Colleen. The incense was a new item, one which I'd hesitated over since I wasn't sure that my typical customer was incense-inclined. Besides, my mother had her own shop in the village, selling crystals and occult items, so I didn't want to compete with the woman who birthed me. But my mom had whipped up a special range of floral and botanical scents especially for Bewitching Blooms, and they'd been surprisingly popular. My favorite was the gardenia, and I pressed it upon anyone who'd listen.

"I imagine you've got quite the garden yourself," Colleen said.

I admitted that my own garden was still a work in progress. "Although my peonies were a triumph this year. I sold a bunch here at the shop. It would be nice if I could do that more often, but time and space can be a challenge." I also failed to mention how Owen Jones, the gardener at Lemmington House, one of Willow Waters' most prestigious homes, was partly responsible for getting those peonies to bloom. But it had been nice to sell some flowers which had been grown just a stone's throw away.

An idea came to me suddenly. "I wonder...if you grow more than you need, then maybe you'd be interested in supplying some for my shop? Of course, I'd need to see the flowers first. But I'd be happy to work out a deal if it's mutually beneficial."

Colleen's eyes widened. She seemed both taken aback and intrigued. I was surprised myself. I normally wasn't so impulsive when it came to decisions about my shop. Or anything, come to think of it. I was more of a sit-back-and-think-about-it kind of gal. A sleep-on-it, never-make-a-decision-on-an-empty-stomach kind of gal. But there was something which drew me to Colleen's garden even though we'd only just met. I'd learned by now to trust my intuition, so I didn't retract the suggestion.

"Now isn't that an idea," she mused, and her eyes began to sparkle.

Now, I'm not judging in the least, but I could almost see the woman mentally calculating how much extra income she could gain if her flowers proved impressive. I appreciated the hustle. We all have to make a living, and goodness knew I had first-hand experience at how hard that could be.

I asked Colleen if I could help her with anything, repeating my opening question with a touch more curiosity now that it was clear she wasn't in the market for a bouquet.

"Gracious," she exclaimed. "With all this talk of business, I'd completely forgotten to tell you why I'm here."

I waited patiently, a smile on my face, but you didn't have to be a witch to figure out why a keen gardener might be paying me a visit since I was going to be judging the garden competition.

And then there it was, that predictable moment. Colleen

pulled out a scrapbook from her rattan carrier and placed it on the worktop with a thud.

"My memory book," she explained, "from the last few years' gardening competitions." She told me she'd heard that I was one of the judges this year and thought I might like to see it. Colleen opened the green leather cover and began to point out her past winning entries. She'd won something every year. "Last year, the competition was in late May, which is a much more sensible time of year, in my humble opinion."

I agreed, of course. The competition had been postponed this year, mostly due to the turbulence of the village needing to acquire a new vicar, among other darker and more unsettling events.

"What's this?" I asked, as Colleen turned the page to reveal a newspaper clipping from *Willower Waters Weekly*. The headline read *Luck of the Iris*.

Colleen giggled. "It's what you call a play on words because I'm Irish and my irises took first prize. Writers are so clever, aren't they?"

I took in the rest of the article. Colleen had beat out three other finalists to the winning prize with her impressive Irish garden, the crowning glory of which were her irises. The article went into great detail about the impressive natural feel of her garden, which was not overly designed or too formal. She had used the natural landscape to dictate elements of the garden with plenty of native Irish plants. They also included some personal details, including how Colleen O'Brien was married to Gabriel O'Brien, and they'd come over from Ireland together twenty years ago and bought the small cottage where they'd worked on the garden ever since. There was a quote from Gabriel saying how proud he was of his wife's green fingers.

"What a write-up," I said to Colleen. "A golden review."

"It was a good year," she said, glowing now. "My husband was instrumental, of course. He does all the heavy work, turning the soil and so on. He's been the muscle and I've been the creative force in the garden for the forty years we've been married."

"Forty years of marriage. Also very impressive."

But at my compliment, Colleen's gaze dropped. "It is. But my Gabriel is back in Ireland at the moment, looking after his mother. She has the Alzheimer's. A terrible disease. It's terrible to be apart, but it's the right thing to do." She sighed. "I do miss him."

My heart went out to Colleen. I knew how difficult it was to be separated from someone you loved and had made your life with. But I couldn't imagine how difficult it would be after so many years of marriage. "Your Gabriel sounds like a good man."

"That he is. Heart of gold, he has. A heart of gold."

I chuckled and thumbed through the rest of Colleen's memory book. There were several touching photographs of Colleen with her husband working in the garden together and standing proudly beside a tiled fireplace whose mantel was covered in trophies. Gabriel was much taller than his wife, with sandy-colored hair, and in every photo his eyes were closed and crinkled, like he'd been caught mid-laugh.

I closed the book with a smile. "Well, this is enough to convince me that you'd be a mighty fine supplier if you have enough flowers to sell." I didn't add *for a fair price, that is*. Some friendly bartering could come later, if it all worked out.

Colleen looked thoughtful. "Judging starts tomorrow, isn't that so? I'm not sure if I'll be on your list, so why don't you come over for a visit anyway and see my flowers yourself? You're welcome any time—whether it's part of the competition or not. You must taste my Irish soda bread."

I was never one to turn down a treat, especially if it went hand in hand with a business opportunity, so I asked Colleen to write down her address and phone number and told her I'd pop by tomorrow after the first meeting of the judges took place, and maybe she'd even be one of the gardens I'd be assigned from our list of entrants. I was fairly certain she was being overly modest when she suggested her garden might not be a finalist.

As she left, Colleen passed Imogen, my floral designer, who was finally returning from what can only be described as a protracted run to Café Roberto's for our usual morning caffeine fix. The two women greeted one another pleasantly, but I knew Imogen's polite smile over her genuine one, and as soon as Colleen disappeared from view, I asked Imogen what was up.

She handed me the black Americano I'd requested and a hazelnut brownie which I hadn't but was grateful to receive. Then she took a seat, flicked back her long blonde hair, and explained that Colleen was well known in the village for her extremely competitive nature. It wasn't limited to gardens. She was also competitive with her knitting circle, her embroidery circle, and at weekly games of bridge.

"My grandmother plays cards with her," Imogen said, biting into her almond croissant. "Colleen drives her crazy but even she can't deny that her garden is gorgeous. She'd just be so much more likable if she didn't grab so many prizes."

"I suppose you do have to have a determined nature to wrangle nature," I said, chuckling at my own pun.

Imogen rolled her eyes. "Determined is the word. She's currently in a bitter feud with her neighbors. They had a large, leafy tree that shaded her garden and dropped leaves. When Colleen complained, they refused to cut it down as they liked it so much and the privacy it provided. But when they were on holiday last Easter, the tree mysteriously died. They believe she killed it, but they can't prove it. Colleen swears it died of some common tree disease."

"Yikes," Norman said, suddenly swooping down from the perch where he'd been napping. "It takes a real meanie to kill a tree. They're the best spots for perching. Maybe you shouldn't go over there, Peony. Do you want to do business with a tree-killer?"

"I already said I'd go. And for all we know, the neighbors' tree could have died a natural death." But I understood Norman's point. I'd try to find out more before buying flowers from Colleen O'Brien.

CHAPTER 2

I was finishing the last of my brownie at my worktable, when Norman said, "Look who's sucking up to the top dog." He was staring out the window, and when I followed his beady gaze, I saw that Colleen O'Brien was talking outside with Alex. She stood closer than necessary, but in truth, I was more interested in looking at Alex than Colleen.

My heart leapt when I saw him, my stomach in knots like a teenager. Even though we'd been spending more time together, getting to know one another, each time I laid eyes on him afresh, I felt a flutter of excitement. My feelings (and his too, I was sure) were growing. But it wasn't exactly a straightforward romance. He was a lord who lived in a castle, an importer of fine wines who also happened to be a werewolf. I was a widowed out-of-towner with supernatural secrets of my own. What future was there for such an odd pairing? No amount of witchy intuition could help me through this one. Though I will admit to you, wherever we did end up, I was enjoying the ride.

But it seemed like I wasn't the only one who was thrilled around Alex.

Colleen appeared to be talking Alex's ear off. Every so often, she squeezed his broad shoulders as if to emphasize a point, and in the brief moments where it seemed as if she were stopping for air, she threw back her head and laughed at whatever Alex was saying. He appeared resigned rather than happy to be speaking with her. Norman's words echoed in my head. Calling him the top dog was right in so many ways. Lord Fitzlupin probably received a lot of attention thanks to his dark good looks, title, and fortune, but I suspected his secret nature added a little animal magnetism to the mix. I definitely felt the pull.

Alex extracted himself from Colleen, crossed the road, and entered my shop.

Imogen looked up from the bouquet she was finishing as he came in with a cool breeze and then grinned when she saw it was Alex.

"Good morning, ladies," he said in his usual charming manner.

I came out from behind the workstation, and he lightly kissed my cheek. A pleasurable shiver went through me.

"I see you were accosted by our last customer," I said, gesturing for Alex to take a seat on one of our stools.

"Colleen O'Brien was in here?" Alex asked.

I nodded. "First time," I replied. "More to do with the gardening competition than the shop. By the looks of it, she had a much nicer time talking with you. Should I be jealous?" I teased.

Alex shuddered.

"That woman's the ultimate social climber," Imogen said,

answering for Alex, who wasn't the kind to speak unkindly about anybody. "She's always trying to ingratiate herself with people she thinks are posh and important. She came in here to get Peony on her side, as she'll be judging the garden competition." Putting her finished bouquet aside, Imogen went to water the hanging baskets outside, and probably to give us some time alone together.

Alex said, "I've agreed to host the prize-giving ceremony at Fitzlupin Castle."

I looked at him in wonder. This was a big deal for the man who, until recently, hadn't let anyone into his enormous ancestral home. Alex was a well-known recluse in the village. His grand castle loomed on the other side of the woodlands from my farmhouse, and apart from his trusted circle, few people gained admittance to the grounds and castle.

That is, until something switched in Alex a few months ago and he began to broaden his horizons and let me into his life. I mean, I couldn't believe it when he approached me for advice on how to host a business client for dinner. Let alone when he invited a London-based team to spruce up his castle and make it look more homely. He'd since been on a furniture-buying binge. And the castle was, happily, slowly starting to look less like a medieval ruin. But that wasn't the only thing to consider.

Even though Imogen was outside, I lowered my voice and asked him if it was safe. It was getting close to a full moon when Alex shifted forms. I knew he asked George to lock him in the castle's dungeon when that happened—he couldn't very well be hosting a soiree the same night.

Alex nodded. "The party itself won't take place on a full moon. I'll be fine. I think it's good for me to integrate more with the community." He smiled. "Besides, now that you're one of the judges, I'd like to support the good-natured competition."

I smiled back. It was so nice watching Alex come out of his shell. I told him I wasn't entirely sure that the competition was all that good-natured, but I was going to give every contestant the benefit of the doubt. Including Colleen O'Brien.

Alex lightly touched my hand. "You've a generous spirit, Peony."

I laughed. "I have?"

"Of course," Alex replied. "Look how you've taken in Char and—" he glanced at where Norman was sleeping on a rafter, "her parrot. Given her the truck. Got her a job. And then there's the shop. You really care about your customers. You even care about lost causes like me."

Was that how Alex really viewed me? I hadn't given much thought to opening up my home to Char. It seemed like the natural thing to do. And he didn't know I was really helping a sister find her way. It was what we did. And I had to argue with another point. "You are not a lost cause," I told him. "In any sense."

"Anyway," Alex said, "I'm working on getting my own gardens improved before the competition officially begins. Not that I'm entering, of course. But now that I'm improving the interior of Fitzlupin Castle, it seems a shame not to beautify the grounds. Though when some of my, ah, friends come over, they tend to dig holes in the dirt."

Alex had never mentioned a pack to me before. I had (maybe naively) assumed he was a lone wolf. I was glad he associated with others of his kind. I'd be totally lost without my coven. Alex must feel the same way. I laid my palm on his arm. "That's great."

"Anyway," he said, sweeping a hand through his black hair. "Just thought I'd say hello and let you know my plans before heading to Café Roberto. He's asked for my opinion on another new brand of coffee bean. The man is quite insatiable when it comes to finding the best coffee in the world."

I laughed and wished him luck. Alex was famous in the village for the many reasons I've already said, but also for his extraordinary sense of smell. It made me chuckle now to imagine what the other Willowers would say if they knew it was because he was part of the canine clan.

He left with the promise of calling later, and I smiled happily to myself, still warm from his affection and kind words.

Imogen waved goodbye as he crossed the street, and I got back to the morning's chores.

Although I was keeping my head down, Norman was determined to keep his beak all the way up. He flapped about and squawked like he was trying to warn me of an impending tornado.

"Goodness, what *is* it?" I said finally after ignoring him failed to halt the performance.

"I'm just so borrrrrred, Cookie," he replied in a whiny teenage drawl. "A guy like me isn't meant to be cooped up like this. I need to spread my wings. I need to soar. I've got important business to attend to."

I snorted.

"You've got to hear me out, Cookie," he continued. "It's not good for my health to be so...sedentary."

I raised my eyebrows, impressed with Normie's vocabulary. Maybe it was from spending time with Hilary at the farmhouse. Those two had become unlikely buddies. I studied Norman's colorful face and saw that his request was earnest. In our desire to keep him from pooping on cars, coffee shop tables, and customers, Char and I had done all we could to tame his wilder instincts. But perhaps he'd learned his lesson by now.

"Maybe you're right," I conceded. "It can't be good for you to nap all day." I peered at his belly. "Plus, you're eating too many treats."

Norman tutted. "Are you suggesting I've piled on the pounds, Cookie? How very dare you."

I laughed. "Would you like to spend more time outside and closer to Char, or not?"

"I'm not waiting for you to change your mind," he said with a huff and promptly flew out of the shop.

I was glad I'd propped open the door—that cheeky bird was so eager to get away he would have flown smack into the glass.

Imogen watched him go, shaking her head. "He is the weirdest creature I have ever met. And that's saying something in Willow Waters."

I smiled and went back to my orders.

It wasn't long before another unfamiliar customer entered the store. Not that I was complaining. I was always pleased to have new business. But as the gentleman came closer, his confident stride and beaming smile telegraphed his intention. This was a salesperson through and through. Imogen knew it, too. She sprang to attention, ready, I could tell, to send the man packing if he was a time-waster. He looked to be in his mid-fifties, dressed in a too-warm suit, pale-pink shirt open at the neck, where dark hairs were matted with sweat. He was carrying a large brown briefcase and glanced between Imogen and me, obviously trying to decide which of us to approach.

"May I help you?" Imogen asked in her most polite, cut-glass voice.

"Good morning, miss," he said, which was not a good start. Imogen was a *Ms.*, thank you very much, as was I, plus she hated anything diminutive which suggested she was young. "I wish to speak to the proprietor of this beautiful shop."

The salesman had a faint European accent I couldn't quite place. "That would be me," I replied, extending a hand. "Peony Bellefleur, owner of Bewitching Blooms. How can I help?"

"Thomas Woolfe," he said, shaking my hand vigorously, "of Woolfeder Gnomes." He smiled again, then explained that he represented a local company and wanted to discuss a potential relationship. "Gnomes," he announced with a flourish, setting his briefcase on my worktop. "It's my family business. We began in my hometown in eastern Germany, and I led our expansion into the southwest of England. I set up production nearby. And I've done my research, Ms. Bellefleur. I know that you sell a wonderful array of gift items. But you are lacking the most noble of all: the garden gnome."

Imogen managed to turn a snort into a cough. I shot her a look. She was being snobbish, and I didn't approve. In fact, I was intrigued. Lots of the cottage gardens in Willow Waters featured a garden gnome or two—sometimes a whole scene —and the gift side of our business was down this quarter, too. I asked Mr. Woolfe to tell me more.

He flashed another smile, took a deep breath, and embarked on his spiel. "You may well think of the humble garden gnomes as just that, Ms. Bellefleur, but let me assure you that is far from the truth. Their history goes as far back as ancient Rome."

He paused for effect, and I mused on the coincidence that a new archaeological dig underway in Willow Waters had recently discovered some ancient Roman artefacts. It would be an excellent talking point in the shop.

He continued to explain that the early Roman gnomes represented their gods and were said to protect the gardens from evil spirits, as well as to ensure a successful harvest. "Since then, the gnome has undertaken many transformations. A Swiss alchemist named Paracelsus was the first one who described them as creatures with magical power. According to him, gnomes were one of the four elementals or nature spirits belonging to the earth. They would come out at night to help plants grow."

At this, Imogen couldn't help but laugh. I shot her another stern look. Luckily, Mr. Woolfe was too engrossed in his own rhetoric to notice. I was finding this fascinating. I wasn't in a position to laugh at nature spirits.

"The popularity of gnomes," he continued, "persisted thanks to the folklore, myths, and stories from around the world such as my very own German fairy tales, where gnomes were often presented as little creatures with mystical power helping humans in farming. They were a good example of how folklore and mythology influenced the history of everyday life. It's widely believed that the very first contemporary-looking garden gnome with the iconic red hat was made by a German sculptor. Soon, the fashion spread across Europe."

He paused, as if waiting for applause. I nodded for him to continue.

"Which is where my family comes in," he said grandly. His face was flushed now, and tiny beads of sweat had gathered at his temples. If Mr. Woolfe made this sales pitch often, I couldn't tell. He spoke with such fervor and vigor, it was as if the words were pouring straight from his heart to our ears. I mean, it was hard to believe the man was talking about gnomes, but to each his own.

"We are one of the few companies who adhere to the traditional methods of gnome-making," he was saying now. "Unlike our competitors, who use plastic or resins, we begin with terracotta clay, using a mold. Once its shape becomes firm, the gnome is removed and set to dry and heat in a kiln. Once ready, we hand-paint the gnomes, usually in bright colors. They are art to us, you see, not nasty plastic things stamped out in a factory."

He paused, waiting again for my reaction. I actually felt inclined to clap, but settled for a nod instead. Mr. Woolfe was an excellent salesman. I was drawn into the story of gnome-making and loved the idea that they were made locally with traditional and non-toxic materials, but I'd have to see for myself.

"Sounds wonderful," I said finally. "Could I see one?"

"But of course," he replied, unclicking his briefcase. "Glad you asked. As you know, the majority of gnomes are shaped as males with long, white beards and pipes. Female gnomes are rather rare, but *we* make them in equal quantities." Lifting the lid of his case, Mr. Woolfe pulled out two gnomes, one male, one female. They were quite charming, with matching yellow overalls and rosy cheeks. The male held a shovel, and the female a watering can.

I was struck by how artistic his gnomes were—not kitsch at all. "These are gorgeous," I said. "They have so much personality."

He thanked me and said, "I think they'd make absolutely perfect gift items in your beautiful shop."

Mr. Woolfe was good. He opened with a compliment and a strong beeline for sales, made his pitch, and then circled back to his opening. I had to admire the skill. But there was something holding me back. I just wasn't sure that I saw gnomes going with cut flowers. They should be in a garden center.

As carefully as I could, I gently put forward my hesitation to Mr. Woolfe. But he wasn't deterred.

"Of course, this is a new idea, and as with all new things, it will take some time getting used to it. There is no hurry, no pressure. Why don't I leave this lovely lady in the shop and you can see what your customers think? A little trial run, as it were. If you get a positive response, which I imagine you will," he paused and his eyes sparkled, "then you can peruse our catalog at leisure." He pushed a thick, glossy brochure across the counter. "You'll see there are many varieties, all more tasteful than others on the market. I hope you'll agree."

I opened the first page and was surprised to see how expensive these gnomes were. Price was the one thing Mr. Woolfe failed to mention.

As if he read my mind, Mr. Woolfe emphasized again that each gnome was handmade and unique. "If you look on the bottom, each gnome has its name engraved, along with the words *Crafted in the UK*. We find our discerning customers enjoy the comfort of knowing where their items are made."

Hmm, after the stinging comment by Colleen O'Brien earlier about bringing in foreign blooms, I decided I'd follow the salesman's suggestion and keep the female gnome by the cash register and see what my own discerning customers thought. Though, after I added a mark-up on top of the wholesale price, these were going to be an expensive purchase. Still, I glanced at the male gnome, who sported a mischievous expression as though he'd play tricks on his friends if they weren't watching, and thought they might be popular with the well-heeled crowd who came to Willow Waters looking for the quaint. They'd certainly find it in those delightful creatures.

I thanked Mr. Woolfe for his time, and he bid me a lovely afternoon.

As soon as he left, Imogen began protesting that the gnomes were expensive and for people with gardens, but I cut her off. "I know, I know, but these gnomes might fill an important gap in our offering. We are in the business of flowers, after all. It's not so different from selling a candle—or local honey. And what do those items have to do with bouquets?"

"They're *classy*," Imogen said.

I picked up the gnome and turned her to face Imogen. "You have to admit, she's very pretty." I studied her carefully painted features, her rosebud lips and wide eyes. "Her name is Yasmin," I read.

I carefully placed Yasmin next to the cash register where she'd hopefully catch the attention of customers and returned to my chores.

CHAPTER 3

$\mathcal{I}$ could never truly keep my head in paperwork at the shop. July was a busy time of year for us, with many of the holiday rentals booking out solidly for the entire month. So, I wasn't surprised when Imogen and I faced an influx of holiday letting agents wanting last-minute bouquets for their clients. Every time I thought the rush was over, a few moments later, another customer would enter. Like I've said before, I was always happy to be busy, but the admin wasn't going to complete itself. It was times like these when part of me wished I could use a spell, but alas—it was against the code. Personal gain was so not cool in the craft. You never knew what might come back to you.

When a jolly voice called out, "Hello, hello!" I glanced up, hoping for a customer this time.

However, the uniform gave away that Willow Waters had a new mailman. His gray shorts were, well, let's just say, on the short side. And his round stomach protruded under his red shirt. With similarly round-framed glasses and a few wisps of gray hair about his otherwise naked head, he came toward me bearing a small stack of letters in his left hand.

"Well, good morning," he said, extending his free hand.

I took it in mine and was treated with a vigorous, enthusiastic shake.

"I'm Marty," he said, "your new postie. I'm looking forward to getting to know you." His voice was warm and full of enthusiasm.

I liked him immediately. I introduced myself, and then Imogen, and we both welcomed him to the village. But before I could ask how long he'd been in town, Marty enquired about my accent. I explained I was born in Maine but had been living here for a few years now. It took Marty less than a second to rattle off a list of facts about Maine and some highlights of a trip he'd taken there fifteen years ago with his wife.

I told him I was glad he liked my homeland. He handed me a sheaf of envelopes and said, "Don't get too excited. It's mostly bills, though there's a letter postmarked California that might be interesting."

I stared at the pile. I didn't know anyone in California. Could an old friend have moved?

"Oh my, isn't she a beauty?" Marty said, before I could look through the mail. He was pointing at the gnome.

I'm not usually one for smugness, but I did feel particularly pleased that it had taken Marty less than a minute to notice Yasmin. No one else had commented on her so far, but then the holiday agents were never really looking at anything when they came in the shop, just ticking off their to-do lists.

"There must be something in the water here, but I've delivered more gnomes in the past week or so than in my whole career! What is it with Willow Waters and gnomes?"

"It might have something to do with the gardening competition next week," I said. "Everyone is in a flurry to add the finishing touches to their gardens." But still, how intriguing that so many of the locals had the same idea. I wondered if it was another example of the competitive nature of this event. One person bought a gnome, thinking it would add something unique, and their neighbor saw it and immediately ordered one and so on.

But Marty didn't reply. He was too busy looking at Yasmin. He picked her up. "This one really has a personality."

I told him I was glad to hear it. "I'm thinking about carrying them as part of my gift selection."

Marty nodded. "They're fine specimens. But a touch too pricey for my humble garden." He bid us goodbye, but stopped again at the door. "If you're friendly with Amanda, be sure to wish her a happy birthday, as from the number of greeting cards I've just delivered to her deli, I'm guessing it's pretty soon."

After he left, Imogen looked as bemused as I felt.

"He's certainly the friendliest mail carrier I've ever met," I said.

"True," Imogen said, "and also the nosiest."

I sorted through the mail and sure enough, Marty was right. Mostly bills. It seemed as though they were coming in thicker and faster than ever these days. The letter with the California stamp was a thank-you note for a delivery ordered by a customer in California who wanted one of our bouquets to be sent to a villager who was recuperating at home after a tricky foot surgery. I was touched by the thoughtful message. They mentioned their friend had recovered quicker than expected after receiving the flowers. I was pleased, as I had imbued the blooms with a little healing magic. There was nothing quite like receiving praise about the shop. I put everything I had into running this place and making sure it was a success. A few words of gratitude meant the world.

"Do you think it's really Amanda's birthday?" Imogen asked.

"I don't know." I turned to Imogen. "Do you mind if I pop over to Amanda's for a moment?"

She shook her head. "Of course not. Especially if you bring back one of her mozzarella focaccias. And wish her a happy birthday from me, too."

I set out to the deli, which was on the other end of the high street.

Amanda's bakery and deli was busy, and I had to wait for a few minutes before my friend was free to speak. I didn't mind—there was nothing more pleasant than perusing her array of chutneys and jams and fresh breads and fine wines. It was a perfect shop. The kind of place I'd want to own if I wasn't so attached to flowers.

Amanda waved me over as soon as she handed the last customer a crusty baguette.

"Peony," she said warmly. "So nice to see you. I feel like it's been ages."

I used to pop into my friend's shop or visit her gorgeous cottage with a bottle of white wine regularly. But now it had probably been three weeks since I'd seen Amanda—I didn't know where the time went. I said as much, and Amanda agreed.

"It's a busy time for all of us in the village. Besides, with a full moon coming up, we'll all be back together soon enough. Personally, I can't wait. I need to tune back into my powers.

It's been so long since I made a healing tonic or even had a spare moment just to collect and macerate the herbs."

I explained that as soon as the gardening competition was over, I was going to be more present with the coven.

Amanda laughed. "I take it no one warned you that the village takes its gardening competition more seriously than its funerals."

I raised an eyebrow. No. No one had warned me—not even my coven sister.

"And Char will be coming again, as usual? To the coven meeting, I mean," Amanda asked as she made the lunchtime sandwiches Imogen had requested.

"Absolutely. Her powers are getting stronger by the month. As soon as she accepted her true nature, it was like she'd given them permission to flow. But wait. I'd completely forgotten the whole reason I came to see you! Is it your birthday this week?"

Amanda buried her face in her hands. "It is. Another one. They come around faster each year."

"No, no, you must celebrate! We'll celebrate you at the meeting. It's perfect timing. Full moon *and* birthday."

I took the sandwiches from Amanda and made a mental note to text the other coven sisters to arrange some kind of birthday surprise.

THE REST of the day passed peacefully, and as I was closing up the shop for the day, Char arrived, looking sweaty and tired—her kohl-rimmed eyes were smudgy and her pink-tipped hair was pulled back into a messy bun.

"I'm exhausted," she said, stating the obvious when I asked how she was doing. "Tourist season is much busier than I imagined. It's doing my head in. People never know what kind of coffee or tea they want. Like, it's not rocket science—it's your personal taste."

I laughed. Char grumbled, but underneath her wannabe rock 'n' roll attitude, she was a softie. And she proved the point by crying out with glee at the sight of Yasmin.

"Isn't she gorgeous!" she exclaimed. "Where did she come from?"

I explained all about our salesman and Yasmin's arrival, and Char agreed with me that selling garden gnomes was a great idea.

I did the final checks and was ready to lock up when Char stopped me. "You can't leave Yasmin alone all night. She's coming with us!" I laughed as Char slotted Yasmin into the front pocket of her denim overalls and we headed to my Range Rover.

Norman was waiting outside, and we piled into my car as Char continued talking about the gnome. "Her face is so life-like. You almost expect her to start talking. Or singing."

Char had obviously decided that today was the day for surprises. As we drove back to the farmhouse, she told me she was eager to learn more magic.

Let me tell you, I nearly crashed us into the nearby lake—the village's signature willows wrapped around my poor Range Rover.

Char, who had accidentally stumbled into Willow Waters en route to London a few months ago, had no idea she was a witch when I met her. In her early twenties, she was escaping a broken relationship and a life controlled by her super-religious parents, who'd dispatched her to the local convent for a strict, pious education. Char rebelled, dyeing the tips of her long brown hair pink, getting a couple of tattoos, and fleeing her home village. Ironically, she ended up in another quiet village where she met the not-so-quiet Norman—her parrot familiar, who spent most of his time irking Char.

The thought made me chuckle now, but Char was aghast when she learned of her true, magical nature. But after a few weeks, and a full moon coven meeting, she began to accept her undeniable powers, especially when it came to lights, fire, and opening doors. Was she ready to learn more?

"That's good, Cookie," Norman said. "It's because you want to spend more time with me. And who wouldn't?"

Char turned in the front seat to face Normie, who was flapping about in the back. "You take some getting used to," she replied.

"Why have you decided now is the time to deepen your practice?" I asked. In my experience, there was a process.

Sure enough, Char said, "I've been dreaming."

"Ah," I said. I knew how dreams could lead us.

"Lately, I've been dreaming of wildfires burning out of control."

I turned to stare at her. "Wildfires?" I scrambled for meaning. Fire was destruction, but it was also one of the four elements. Warmth, light, and power were all associated with fire, so long as you handled it carefully. But an out-of-control fire was terrifying.

She nodded. "They aren't scary. The fires were beautiful. Vivid oranges, burnt sienna, golden flames. They burned brightly and with an intensity that both awed and overwhelmed me."

I asked her where the fires took place, but Char only shrugged. "It's not a specific place. I don't recognize it. Sometimes I think they're in the woodlands here. Other times, they feel like they're coming from another realm. I don't get it."

It was a good sign that she wasn't afraid, but her subconscious was telling her something. "There's a message in there somewhere. We need to work out what it means."

"Good. But I think they are telling me to get more involved in magic." She paused. "Or maybe I'm afraid that if I don't learn more of the craft, I won't be able to protect us from the fire."

"They're only dreams," I reassured her, but inside I felt a bit nervous too.

We spent the rest of the ride home enjoying the early evening breeze, which blew in through the open windows and ruffled my hair as well as Char's—and Normie's bright feathers, too. Early July brought with it a host of new green and floral scents which traveled on that gentle wind, and I felt calm after a long day at work, looking forward to spending some time in my garden before the light went.

After a busy day and Char's surprising announcement, I felt a little garden time would help me think.

CHAPTER 4

I parked the Range Rover and the three of us headed 'round the back of the farmhouse. Hilary, my other lodger, was on cooking duty tonight, which always meant a delicious dinner. Char was planning a barbecue when it was her turn. To be honest, Char was probably most interested in seeing whether she could get the BBQ going using her newfound fire powers. But Hilary was an ordinary woman and any talk of magic had to take place away from her astute ears.

I say she was ordinary, but Hilary had her own special qualities. A happily divorced ex-barrister, Hilary had left the world of law behind and was studying Classics as a mature student. She'd been in a particularly good mood this week as Willow Waters was currently home to an archaeological dig —and she'd struck up a firm new friendship with Dr. Dawn Fanning, a renowned archaeologist with a well-regarded television show, here to cover the dig.

But when I arrived home, Hilary had left a note saying she was at the butcher.

Char rushed out to the garden and placed Yasmin next to a particularly fragrant patch of stocks. I had to admit that the gnome looked picturesque in her temporary home. But watching Char talk to her as if she were real was slightly alarming.

At this time of year, my garden should have been in full swing. I knew that many gardens could peak in early July, especially if they were planted with lots of veggies. But after my conversation with Colleen about her award-winning garden, I was looking at my own with a more critical eye. I'd recently laid a new stone path which led to the woodland behind the house and, as I told you earlier, Owen Jones, gardener extraordinaire, had given me a helping green hand with a few trimmings here and there. Certain parts of the garden were thriving: delphiniums, clematis, which climbed the wood fences, the lavender borders, and honeysuckle all combined to fill the air with scents. It was a beautiful garden in my eyes, fragrant and a little wild.

Yet I'd neglected several important jobs. July was a time for deadheading the flowering plants. For most blooms, this meant snipping away at the spent ones, and I'd neglected the roses and achillea. My patch of sweet peas was also floundering. To keep them at their best, they needed regular attention, which mostly entailed picking and picking and picking some more, which encouraged the plant to keep producing blooms. The plant should keep flowering all summer, but if I didn't get to work, they wouldn't even make it to August.

A judge of the local garden competition couldn't be letting herself down this way. I would have to work harder. Maybe call in another favor with Owen. I was sure he'd be glad to help with Char nearby. Those two liked being around one another far more than either let on.

"What are you groaning about?" Normie said as he swooped down from a nearby branch.

I told him I was lamenting my subpar garden. But I shouldn't have expected Norman to understand. His only response was to point out how many good places there were for perching. Of course.

I fetched the clippers from the garden shed and as I set to work, I asked Char what she'd like to learn next in her magical education.

She'd stretched out on one of the red and white loungers, watching Yasmin the gnome settle in to her temporary home. I had to admit, the gnome already looked at home.

"Opening doors and sparking light with my fingertips is fine and all, but what I really what is to bring things to life."

A shudder went through me, and I stared at Char in horror. "That's dark magic. You must *never* try to bring something back from the dead."

Char laughed. "I'm not talking dead people, Peony. I meant Frodo."

I breathed a sigh of relief. Frodo was Char's previously broken-down Citroën truck. It had belonged to Jeremy, my late husband, who had never managed to get the old thing running in his too-short lifetime. Char was naturally mechanically gifted and had the truck purring in an incredibly short time.

"I want to learn how to start Frodo without using the keys."

I raised a brow. "I'm not surprised, given how often you misplace them."

"Inside the fridge, under the bed, in my water bowl, in the ignition," Norman said, listing the bizarre places we'd discovered Char's keys—either dropped or carelessly set down.

With my heartbeat steady now, I agreed to help Char. "There's a spell we can try. And it'll work for any engine for which you already have an affinity." If there was such a thing as a mechanical witch, that's what Char was.

I gathered three candles from the kitchen and set them in a circle on the green lawn. We could get started while Hilary was out. I motioned for Char to sit and for Norman to stay quiet. As he was Char's familiar, her powers were stronger when he was nearby, but he also needed to not interfere—a tough ask for a chatty bird.

"Don't we need to be near the truck for this to work?" she asked, frowning.

"Patience, patience," I chided. "First, you need to get into the right headspace. Like it or not, you're full of emotion and fire, Char, and for a spell to work, you need to empty out surplus feeling to become a conduit for the magic."

"I'm not that deep," Char argued.

I smiled. Char *was* that deep—she just didn't like to admit it. Far too uncool for her liking.

Char got off the lounger and came to sit on the grass. She crossed her legs, and I instructed her to close her eyes. She glared at me with her usual defiant posturing, but I waited, and she soon obeyed and let her eyelids flutter closed. I began to guide her through a meditation to focus her mind.

"The past has gone, and the future is yet to come. Concentrate on being peaceful, happy, and free in this present moment."

Char let out a loud, exaggerated sigh. "I could find this on a YouTube video about meditation," she said.

I continued, ignoring her reluctance. Control came from the mind as well as the body. Char needed to learn how to be still. Of course, this was like meditation. Essentially, that's what we were doing to calm her mind.

"Concentrate on being aware of each breath. Follow it as the breath begins, feel your abdomen start to expand, then how it rises and falls with each breath."

I watched Char's face. As much as she liked to put on a hard front, I could see that she was attempting to follow my instructions. Maybe a little too earnestly—she was screwing up her face with concentration. But I'd take it.

"Imagine your abdomen like a child on a swing going high and low."

At that, Char's eyes flicked open, and she laughed.

I tutted, sounding a lot like Norman, who was thankfully on the other side of the garden chirping around Blue, my marmalade cat, who had emerged from the farmhouse to welcome us home. Those two had become unlikely friends. Blue so sassy in her silence; Normie so, well, Normie. But they seemed to enjoy each other's company and having both our familiars present while Char worked on a new spell would only increase its power.

I instructed Char to close her eyes again, and this time I simply asked her to focus on the idea of staying in the here and now. No running, no scheme, no moving forward. Just stillness. Char responded to my words, and I watched with pleasure as her shoulders finally relaxed and dropped, her mouth and jaw slackened. All her tension dissolving. She actually looked peaceful, though the charge coming off her body was electric.

I kept reminding Char to breathe in through her nose and out through her mouth, to concentrate on each breath, and for a full five minutes, she stayed completely still. What was going on in her mind was another matter entirely, and I figured I didn't really want to know. But at least her body was relaxing. This way, she would be more receptive to her powers. A better conduit for magic. When I could feel she was relaxed and present, I told her to open her eyes.

"Namaste," she said, folding her hands into prayer position and bowing in an exaggerated fashion.

I wanted to laugh, but stopped myself. She might make fun of the process, but I knew how important it was.

Now, I told her, it was time to tackle Frodo. I picked up the three, as yet unlit, candles from the grass and followed Char to the outbuilding she'd taken over as a garage. "Wait," I called out. "I almost forgot my mom's crystals." I ran back to the kitchen where I kept them.

What? Doesn't everyone keep their healing crystals one drawer down from the wooden spoons? I guess it helps that my mom is a medium, communing daily with the dearly departed, and the proud proprietor of Willow Waters' (only) crystal and occult shop. With my mom's training, I knew the power of the right crystal when casting a spell, so I selected red carnelian, a stone of fire. Then I grabbed a tarot deck before joining Char in the garage.

Our two familiars followed me, obviously sensing that they were needed. Excellent.

I found Char lovingly polishing Frodo's wing mirror.

"Right," I said, "first job is to light these." I gestured at the candles which I'd set in a circle.

"Easy-peasy," she said, and with a flick of her wrist, all

three wicks ignited simultaneously.

"Impressive." I'd never seen her light more than one thing on fire. She was demonstrating great control already. It felt like only yesterday I'd discovered Char sitting outside the farmhouse, shaking, because fire had spontaneously started coming out of her fingertips. I pulled the Strength card from the tarot deck and placed it in the circle.

Char studied the card with its image of a lion and a woman—her expression calm and gentle yet clearly dominant over the lion. I placed the crystals around the tarot card, making a smaller ring inside the candles.

"Now what?" Char asked.

"Now hold the intention in your mind. Picture Frodo's engine firing up. Hear its rumble. And now, we chant."

I asked Char to close her eyes and felt the words of a spell form unaided in my mind.

> *From air to water, fire to earth,*
> *Give this engine a new birth,*

I asked Char to pick up the chant and to raise her hands toward the center of the circle. Her usually smooth forehead wrinkled in concentration. I'd never seen her so focused.

> *Let my intention be the key.*
> *So I will, so mote it be.*

She repeated the whole spell again. And again.

After a couple of minutes, the candle flames began to flicker and tremble. I silently willed Char to double her efforts. Something was happening. I could feel it in the air.

Char's eyes flashed open, and she let out a cry of frustration.

"No," I murmured. "Stay in the moment."

"Nothing's happening," she whined. "I'm trying so hard."

"You didn't see it, but the flames started to waver. The charge is in the air. I'm sure Frodo is going to pick it up soon."

Char pouted, but closed her eyes again and picked up the words of the spell. I was silently repeating the same words, adding my power to hers. Norman was perched on a rafter in the roof while Blue had jumped up onto an old cabinet where Char kept tools and was sitting watching us, her tail occasionally flicking.

Suddenly, Frodo began to splutter to life. Not exactly an engine purring, more like a wet battery trying to turn over. A cough and then silence. But it was something!

Char opened her eyes. "Now we're getting somewhere," she said, clapping her hands together. "I can't believe I just did that!"

"I can." It was so nice to see Char getting excited about her powers and willing them to grow. I had a strong intuition that the future was going to be bright for Char, hopefully as bright as the fire she controlled with her fingertips.

Char tried a couple more times to start Frodo, but with no luck.

"Try again tomorrow," I said. "When you're fresh."

She agreed, and I could see how much her small success had ignited her own engine.

Even Normie was impressed. He swooped down to land on her shoulder. "Nice going, Cookie," he said, and gave her a loving nibble on her earlobe.

CHAPTER 5

*W*hen Char and I returned to the farmhouse, Hilary had returned from the butcher and begun dinner and the smell of roasting chicken wafted through the kitchen.

My mom, Jessie Rae, was fluttering around the kitchen as was her way, tossing her red ringlets over her shoulders, getting in Hilary's way. Mom was here so often, she might as well have lived with us. Instead, she insisted on living independently of me. I had no idea who she thought she was fooling. She had a key of her own, a room of her own, and she preferred eating dinner at the farmhouse but categorically refused just to make the thing official and move in.

Let me tell you a thing or two about my lodger Hilary. As I've already mentioned, she was a retired lawyer and history buff, and Classics was her area of passion. In fact, I didn't know quite how passionate Hilary could be until Willow Waters became home to its very own archaeological dig at the famous Barnham House. A listed manor house dating back to the Tudor period, Barnham House was famous for its gorgeous gardens, part of which were now the subject of an archaeological excavation.

I lightly touched Hilary on the back as she de-podded a broad bean from the pile on her favorite chopping board. Yes, Hilary had a favorite chopping board—she was the head chef of the house, after all.

"Looks yummy," I said, as she added the fresh beans to a huge green salad. "From the garden?"

Hilary nodded. "Picked them yesterday and almost forgot all about it. You did a grand job growing these. And the rosemary for the chicken was from the garden too."

I felt a spurt of pride. My garden *did* have its highlights.

"Peony, lassie," my mom said, flitting over to kiss my cheeks. "I've been thinking about you all day."

Jessie Rae was wearing a particularly impressive ensemble of an orange and gold smock paired with burgundy leggings and gold sandals, which showed off her painted toes. Her bangles jingled as she drew back from me.

"Good things, I hope?"

"Ay, well, strange things."

Char emitted an almost inaudible groan from the kitchen table where she was setting our places for dinner. I felt the usual mild alarm at my mom's cryptic communication. One of her visions was bound to be at the center of this.

"It was the vision I had, you see," Mom said, and I fought against the urge to roll my eyes. I didn't need to encourage her to go on. Jessie Rae loved to tell people about the visions which appeared to her and only her. Sometimes they were straightforward, other times so cryptic that it would take a team of specialists of various professions to work out.

"I saw you as a young lassie, with a crown of daisies atop that wee bonnet of yours."

"Bonnet, like a car bonnet?" Char piped up.

"No, lassie," my mom corrected. "Bonnet as in your head. I saw Peony here as a young girl with a crown of daisies around her head. Strange thing was, she was surrounded by little people."

Hilary gulped down a laugh. "Little people?"

"Do you mean like fairies?" I asked. This was definitely proving to be one of my mom's more eccentric visions.

Char snorted.

"Hmm, they weren't fairies, but they were that small. I couldn't figure it out. The mood of the vision wasn't menacing, just off-kilter. Something was up and it bothered me all day."

"You know, Mom, instead of being distracted all day, you could have just texted me to see if I was okay? That is one of the more obvious conveniences of modern living."

But my mom just flipped her red curls back over her shoulder again. She didn't care for contemporary means of communication—she was more about vibes and attempts at telepathy.

"Well, I can see with my own eyes you're absolutely fine, lassie. Just maybe beware of daisies at the shop. Or anything that looks like a miniature person."

The only thing in my world like a miniature person was the garden gnome. Perhaps the spirits were telling me they were too expensive to bother stocking in my shop. I had a feeling the spirits might be right.

I carried Hilary's giant green salad to the table. She added a plate of roasted chicken, baked with rosemary and lemon, a pot of mayonnaise, and a homemade garlic baguette, still warm from the oven. It was perfection.

Hilary said, "I heard the truck engine struggling to start. Everything all right with the truck?" She was too elegant to call him Frodo.

I shot Char a warning look, but I needn't have worried. Acting nonchalant was second nature to Char.

"Just tuning up the engine," Char said.

It was enough to shut down any further questions, but to my surprise, Hilary said how lucky Char was to have mechanical abilities.

Char looked gratified by the compliment and told us that in fact she'd been approached by several customers at Café Roberto where she worked, who'd heard she could fix vehicles. "I could make some extra money. Bit of a side hustle," she said with pride.

I was glad Char was earning a good reputation in the village. As I've explained before, Willowers weren't exactly all-embracing of outsiders and Char wasn't always the warmest of characters. She was an excellent barista, and now she was becoming known for her other skills as well.

After complimenting Hilary on her perfectly roasted chicken, I asked her if she'd heard from Dawn.

Dawn Fanning was the renowned archaeologist who presented the television show *Digging into History* and who, having heard about the Barnham House discovery, had arrived in Willow Waters with her production company looking for a new project. As part of her show, Dawn had joined the archaeologist team, making plans for how to excavate further.

It was a complicated site because the gardens and house

were historic and protected by law, but there was evidence of a historic site beneath the celebrated gardens. Although it was still early days, the dig team had already unearthed bits of mosaic tile, likely from a Roman villa, plus pot shards and Roman coins. Dawn had told us in confidence that there were also animal bones and older coins, so they weren't sure yet how far back the site went.

It was amazing to me how long objects could lie undisturbed, keeping the stories of the human beings who owned them secret for hundreds, even thousands of years.

The whole village was excited to play host to a TV crew and to be at the center of such a historic site. But no one was more excited than Hilary, whose very lifeblood ran with history. She had struck up a firm friendship with Dawn almost instantly. I was pretty pleased with myself, as I was the one who introduced them.

Hilary grinned. "Why yes, she messaged me just this afternoon to see if I wanted to join the archaeological team for the pub quiz at The Mermaid this week."

Jessie Rae gasped. "But you can't! You're on our team. You supply the history knowledge. We need you."

Hilary looked torn. Obviously she was thrilled to be invited into the inner circle of the archaeology buffs, but she was also loyal—even if it was to a motley crew like us.

I gently hushed my mom and served her some more salad. "We can release Hilary from our team for one month, Mom. She deserves to spread her wings. Besides, it'll spice up the competition. We can ask someone else in the village to make up our numbers."

Jessie Rae was clearly unhappy about losing our best team member, but tucked into her salad all the same.

"How's the garden competition coming?" Hilary asked, no doubt to change the subject. "Have you had your first meeting with the committee?"

Char rolled her eyes. She couldn't contain her boredom at even the briefest of mentions of the garden competition. She was interested in carburetors, not chrysanthemums. I watched with amusement as she focused all her attention on the crusty garlic bread.

"No. We're meeting tomorrow. But wow, people are eager. I met one of the previous winners just this morning. If you ask me, her visit was letting me know, as a new judge, that she's a serious contender."

"I coulda been a contender," Normie quoted from his perch.

I have to say, his Brando impression wasn't bad. For a parrot.

"Who was it?" Hilary asked.

I explained about my conversation with Colleen O'Brien, who had arrived at the shop this morning with zero intention of buying flowers but instead to show me her memory book of garden competition wins. "Apparently, she's famous for her irises. After she left, Imogen told me she's wildly competitive, which I'd pretty much figured out.
"

"What a cheek," Hilary said.

"I know. But I tried to look on the bright side—if she's that skilled at growing flowers, she might be able to supply me with some local blooms for the shop. I'm going to visit her garden."

Hilary swallowed and then put down her fork. "Imogen's not wrong. I know Colleen. She's prouder of her garden than most women are of their children." She raised a disapproving eyebrow.

"Well, I'm not here to judge her character—just her flowers," I said, shrugging. "I'm sure I'll learn more at the first meeting of the judges."

Hilary laughed. "Truly, I don't think you know what you've agreed to."

Suddenly, the dishwasher door sprang open, cutting Hilary off in mid-chuckle.

Hilary leapt to her feet. "What on earth was that?" She walked over to the dishwasher and peered into its depths like it might answer her question.

Char grabbed my hand across the table, and then I knew.

You? I silently mouthed.

She nodded and mouthed back, *Accident.*

We'd made progress, but her powers were still too haphazard for random experiments with home appliances. I'd have a word with her later when we were alone.

While Hilary fussed with the dishwasher, Jessie Rae whispered, "It's a full moon soon, lassie. Make sure your head isn't too full of the garden competition to prepare."

I didn't understand why she was so concerned. So what if the two events were close together? I whispered as much, but Jessie Rae just shook her head again, making her curls ripple against her shoulders.

I swiftly changed the conversation to the subject of dishwasher repairs. But still, there was something unnerving about my medium mother worrying about the upcoming full moon. I knew the full moon could bring out undesirable traits in people. But surely it wouldn't affect something as benign as a garden competition.

Could it?

CHAPTER 6

The next morning brought a glorious sunrise that I witnessed as I opened my bedroom curtains. Blue, my sleepy ginger familiar, mewed softly at the unwelcome disruption of her lavish snooze. Before Blue, I had thought all cats were crepuscular—most active at dusk and again at dawn. But no. My Blue was the exception to the rules of the natural world. She slept through any time of day. The only time she became energetic was when she felt like I was in danger. Or if I needed the strength of our bond to help with a spell.

I couldn't complain, though it would be nice to have the bed to myself every once in a while. Blue was a terrific snorer.

I donned my slippers and a silk kimono-style dressing gown before padding downstairs. It was early, too early to have to get up on a Saturday morning, but Arthur Higgins-bottom, who chaired the garden competition committee, had decided it would be 'delightful' to have our first meeting early Saturday morning when he'd assign which gardens we'd each visit. Then we'd do the first round of judging.

It was all right for him. He was retired, but I had a shop to run and Saturdays were busy. But then every day was busy for me except Sunday, and the vicar, Justine Johnson, was obviously unavailable on Sunday mornings. So, I sucked it up and rose earlier than I needed to.

Imogen would open Bewitching Blooms, and since Char didn't have to work at Roberto's, she'd agreed to help out for the extra money. She couldn't arrange a bouquet, but she could run the till and deliver flowers in Frodo, so it was a good solution.

I'd head to work later. But first, coffee.

In the kitchen, I brewed coffee and set about preparing Blue's breakfast. She might be snoozy, but that girl could eat, and if her breakfast wasn't ready and waiting when she deigned to rouse herself, then the meowing would be horrendous.

Despite my annoyance at being up so early, I did like this time of day. It was unusual for me to be awake before Hilary —who considered sleep an inconvenient interruption to her reading schedule—and I rarely had the kitchen to myself. The sound of chattering birds was loud enough to penetrate the French doors, and with my coffee brewed, I went to open them, welcoming the song and the particular optimism it inspired.

Imagine my surprise when I saw someone at the back of my garden. Good thing I loved coffee too much to drop the cup. Of course, you might be thinking *intruder! Intruder! Why isn't she reciting a spell for danger?* But don't worry—something about the figure was familiar. I wasn't fazed for long. In fact, I quickly felt comforted, like someone was watching over me.

Stepping out onto the patio, I raised my free hand to

shield my eyes against the rising sun. The figure slowly came into focus. Of course, I'd felt only surprise and no sense of danger. It was Owen Jones, the gardener from Lemmington House and a friend to our whole household. He'd been helping out in my garden, too, but we hadn't arranged an appointment. Why was he here?

I called his name and waved. Owen stopped whatever he was doing and walked toward the patio, a cap slung low across his brow. I noticed the blue shadows beneath his eyes and guessed he was here because he'd been having trouble sleeping and wanted to do something more useful than staring at the ceiling.

"Morning," I said. "You're up early."

"Couldn't sleep," Owen said, confirming my guess. "Thought I'd plant those fennel seeds I was telling you about. Found the perfect spot in your vegetable patch. Any later and we would have missed the window."

I thanked him, knowing better than to pry into whatever was bothering him. Owen was a private man who was trying to keep his head down and work hard after a stint with a bad crowd back in his hometown in Yorkshire. He knew that I was keen to grow more of my own vegetables, and since he often had seeds and bulbs left over from his work, he made sure they didn't go to waste.

"Hilary will be so happy," I said. "She loves fennel."

Owen nodded. "Nothing tastes as good as when you grow it yourself."

I offered Owen a cup of coffee, but he shook his head, saying he'd best get back to the big house and start the day's work. "You're off to the rectory this morning, I take it."

I was surprised Owen knew and said as much.

Owen just laughed. "Don't be shocked. The gardening competition is all anyone can talk about." His eyes twinkled. "And you know I have a stake in it, too."

I did. And it worried me. The gardens at Lemmington House were exquisite. No one could say otherwise. But I was concerned that the villagers might object to the owner entering her garden in a competition when everyone knew she hired a gardener to do all the work. All kinds of village politics had risen to the surface since I'd agreed to help judge the competition.

"I see you've succumbed to the new fashion in garden gnomes," he said, pointing to Yasmin, who looked as though she'd enjoyed her night in my garden.

Her lips were as fresh and dewy as strawberries, and her yellow outfit gleamed.

I told him I was thinking of selling garden gnomes like Yasmin in my shop and that her kind were made locally.

He nodded. "At least you're stocking the decent ones."

Owen excused himself to finish his planting, and I thanked him again before heading inside to make a snack before the meeting.

I almost jumped out of my skin when I saw Char sitting at the kitchen table, flicking through a car magazine. "You're up early," I exclaimed.

"Couldn't sleep," Char said, yawning to prove her point.

"Must be something in the air," I murmured and explained that Owen was in the garden, complaining of the same malady. I held myself back from saying that it was just another thing those two had in common.

Living with Char these past few months meant I knew what pushed her buttons, and she certainly did not like being the subject of speculation. If Owen and Char were ever to realize their feelings for one another, it wouldn't be because someone else had pointed it out.

And yet Char slowly put down her magazine and let her gaze settle on the garden. I anticipated a look of pleasure as she spied Owen, but Char suddenly leapt to her feet.

"What's wrong?" I asked, as the color drained from Char's already pale face.

"Nothing. I thought I saw Normie about to poop near Owen."

I frowned, unconvinced. There was no way Norman would do anything to upset Owen. I assumed Char was just crushing on the gorgeous gardener but was surprised by the depth of her reaction.

And yet her expression, still staring out into the garden, was unnerving.

A SMALL PLATE of eggs and a hot shower later, I retrieved Yasmin from the garden, packed the car, and made my way to the rectory for the first meeting of the Willow Waters Prettiest Garden Judging Committee. I had never been inside the modest rectory next to the village church and was curious to see inside the home of our new vicar, Justine. I do love a good old cottage.

From the outside, the rectory was unassuming. A simple rectangular stone building, it was built almost a hundred years later than our fourteenth-century church, but with equal amounts of charm. An iron portico with curling pink roses marked the entrance and beyond stood a heavy wooden door. The front garden was a colorful array of pansies and sweet peas. I wondered if Justine knew more about flowers than she let on.

Justine opened the door, greeting me with a warm smile. She was wearing a green floral dress and appeared more well-rested than I felt. I had warmed to Justine the moment I'd met her and was pleased that we were embroiled in this competition together. I had the feeling I was going to need the moral support.

She led me through a dark hallway to the kitchen at the back of the rectory. This room was flooded with light, and I saw my fellow judges had already assembled. As I said before, we were a strange bunch. I wasn't sure who'd decided that a florist, a vicar, an organist, and the head of a local history society would make a good garden judging panel, but so it had been decreed and so it must be.

Arthur sat at the head of the table on an elaborate wooden love seat, which my mom would have loved to stock in her shop. Arthur's strands of gray hair were neatly combed to one side. His eyebrows were much darker, reddish in tone, and quite bushy. He was a little overweight and wore a loose pale-yellow shirt with a handkerchief poking out from the chest pocket. He shuffled a stack of papers and spread a few across the table.

Since he had judged before, he had also taken it upon himself to chair this committee. Well, that was fine by me. The responsibility of judging was enough. Arthur impressed me with his ability to be both mild-mannered and almost fanatical about local history.

To his left was Bernard Drake, the wonderful church organist. A retired music teacher, he was calm, well-organized, and well-liked by the entire community. Even my mom (who tended not to have any opinion on anyone actually living, preferring to focus her attention on those dearly departed) liked Bernard and what she dubbed his pink and loving energy. He was wearing his usual uniform of tweed trousers and golfing top that paid no heed to the warm weather.

Only then did it occur to me that anyone in the village who was an expert on gardens would likely enter the competition. No doubt that's how we'd ended up with this assortment of judges.

"Have a seat, Peony," Justine said.

My gaze was immediately drawn to the table where she'd put on an amazing spread. A plate of croissants sat next to pots of glistening jam, sliced melon, and brown rolls piled high—a selection of cheeses and charcuterie beside it. I began to regret having eaten my plate of scrambled eggs. But who didn't love a second breakfast?

"I thought a little meal would help us concentrate and fuel us for the day ahead. But I got carried away at Amanda's deli."

I completely understood. It was easy to do.

Justine offered me a coffee, and as I took a seat next to Bernard, she poured a steaming cup. I looked around the room, each corner revealing a new and pleasing detail. Although I had kept my farmhouse renovation sympathetic, it was clear that the rectory was almost entirely untouched by time. Many vicars must have come and gone throughout the years, but Justine had put her stamp on the place with a few paintings that I suspected belonged to her rather than the church. She liked modern, abstract art. And on the kitchen counter was a set of pottery canisters in the shapes of farm animals. It was whimsical and homey.

I simply adored the ancient stone flooring and exposed beams, though I imagined Justine would paint the place from its uniform beige if she stayed long enough.

Arthur said, "It's a shame Barnham Gardens can't be considered this year as it is the site of an archaeological dig which has been greenlit at Barnham House and is being filmed for the TV show *Digging into History*." We all knew this, but I got the feeling he just liked saying the words.

"Will you be part of it?" Justine asked.

He'd have told us anyway, so it was kind of her to give him an opening. Though I wanted to get on with the meeting and my day.

I reached for a croissant.

"Glad you asked, Justine," he said, a wide smile spreading across his face. "Since I'm considered to be something of a local expert, I expect the team on *Digging into History* will be after an exclusive interview with me. I've been *very* busy writing notes." He cleared his throat. "How does this sound? Willow Waters is well known for its rich legacy of Roman and pre-Roman history and much of the original Roman infrastructure remains today. Did you know the soil was sown with salt by the early Romans after they successfully conquered and razed new lands?"

"Sown with salt?" Bernard asked with a bemused expression.

"It's the custom of purifying or consecrating a destroyed city with salt and cursing anyone who dared to rebuild it. Well, I *am* taking some poetic license with that statement as, of course, the soil around here isn't actually *salty* per se.

Otherwise we wouldn't have so many lovely gardens. Perhaps I should make it more mysterious. A reference to how a beautiful bed of flowers and lawn can hide the dramas, wars, and plagues of history."

"Very compelling," Justine said, taking the seat opposite me.

"In a way, it's a shame we're convening to discuss what grows on top of the earth rather than what's buried beneath it."

He'd given Justine the opening she needed. "But, since we're here to talk about gardens, let's begin."

CHAPTER 7

ustine, used to leading an entire parish, swiftly redirected the garden competition committee's attention to the matter at hand. "I'd like to open our first official meeting with a discussion about the practicalities of judging. As a newbie to the process, I do wonder how we're going to get around to so many entries. What's the final number, Arthur?"

"Eighteen," he replied.

"Wow," I said. "There are a lot of proud gardeners." It was a surprisingly high number, considering how small a village we were.

"I'll say," Bernard agreed. "But we'll divide the visits, document the gardens with photographs, and record our thoughts on score sheets to narrow it down to a shortlist. From there, we'll all visit the lucky few and choose the final three."

I could see now why everyone in the village was taking the competition so seriously. It was a real process! On top of that, every entry came with a fee, which was how we raised the prize money as well as some cash to go back into the community. This year, the remaining funds were being used to repaint the church hall and plant a new tree in the local woodland.

"What are the prizes for the final three?" Justine asked.

"The winner receives a gift certificate for Ray's Sunny Garden Centre," Arthur said, "but second and third place have yet to be decided. We like to get businesses to donate prizes in exchange for publicity." Arthur fixed his eyes on me. "Perhaps it might be nice if your shop donated a bouquet for second place?"

"I could come up with something," was my response. Was this the real reason I'd been invited onto the judging committee?

As though reading my mind, Justine added, "And perhaps I'll offer a prayer about the sin of pride."

I snorted. Justine's sense of humor was a breath of fresh air in a meeting which was staider than I could have ever imagined. She shot a playful yet poignant look at Arthur, who remained oblivious.

"Perhaps a certificate and a gardening book might provide a fair prize?" Bernard suggested. "I know that the church receives many donations, books among them, and lots are in pristine condition. We could wrap them up in a nice bundle?"

Justine clapped her hands. "An excellent suggestion."

At Justine's insistence, I helped myself to another croissant and a slice of melon.

"Speaking of books," I said after swallowing a delicious mouthful of melon, "I had Colleen O'Brien in my shop yesterday. She brought along her memory book."

The words 'brag book' had been about to slip from my

mouth, but luckily I'd halted their trajectory before it was too late.

"She's quite the enthusiast." Secretly, I expected Colleen was already practicing her winner's speech, but I kept that thought to myself.

"Oh, Colleen's garden is one of the glories of Willow Waters," Arthur said.

"Yes," Bernard agreed. "Her irises are something to behold. Quite exceptional. When she does the flowers for the church, they are always exceptional."

I was struck by how, every time I mentioned Colleen in conversation, everyone knew who she was and had an opinion about her. Some more positive than others.

"Plus, she has the most wonderful collection of gnomes I've ever seen," Bernard added.

Now that took me aback. "Really?" I asked. "I didn't notice any in her scrapbook."

Bernard nodded. "New additions this year. Perhaps they're coming into fashion again. Stranger things have happened. I'm quite fond of the little fellows myself."

I smiled, pleased that my instincts about Yasmin and her family of artisan gnomes had been right. It might just be exactly what Bewitching Blooms needed to increase business.

Arthur set about dividing the gardens between us at random. We were each assigned four gardens and then, as the senior judges, Arthur and Bernard each took an extra. Arthur handed out his personally-designed judging score sheets and instructed us to take several clear photographs of each garden on our phones. The first round of judging would start straight away.

I swallowed, wondering again if I had bitten off more than

I could chew with this competition. If Colleen O'Brien was anything to go by, emotions were about to run high. I was more curious than ever to see her garden.

Fortuitously perhaps, when the lists of gardens were assigned, Colleen was on mine. So, too, was her neighbors'. At least that minimized my driving around town. I recalled again how Imogen said Colleen was engaged in some ugly backyard politics with the couple next door.

Was Colleen simply a keen gardener with a passionate streak?

Or was she vindictive enough to poison a tree?

BY THE TIME we'd finished the meeting, it was after nine and the official judging had opened. All the gardeners had been asked to stand by between nine and five today, knowing one of the judges would show up, though they didn't know which one. No time like the present, I thought (aka, let's get this over with).

I thought I'd visit three gardens this morning, join Imogen at the shop for the busy rush, and then hit my last garden in the late afternoon. To say I had my work cut out for me was an understatement. Thank goodness I was fueled with two good breakfasts.

I checked my list. Elizabeth Sanderson was closest, so I'd head to her place first. I also thought she'd be a good person to begin with. Elizabeth lived in a cottage by the high street and was the president of the local chapter of the Women's Institute. She was a nice lady, always composed, with a sweet, kindly face and carefully coiffured blonde hair. She was a renowned embroiderer and the kind of person who had lace curtains at the windows, always clean and starched. I was intrigued to see what might lie behind that neat exterior. Was she going to surprise me with a wild meadow-like garden?

You could never predict this kind of thing. Take Alex, for example. I never would have guessed that the interior of his beautiful castle was sparsely furnished and run-down. Although all that was changing now and he was set on making it a real home.

Elizabeth's home was snug in the middle of a row of classic Cotswold cottages, which gave Willow Waters its picture-postcard reputation. From a distance, each one looked alike with its pale stone and lead-piped windows. But on closer inspection, each owner had stamped their personality on their property in as many ways as possible. Elizabeth had painted her front door pistachio green, and it was flanked on either side with hanging baskets bursting with pansies and ivy. When I drew up and parked outside, Elizabeth opened the door.

I gave Elizabeth a friendly wave, and she lit up as I approached. I don't mind telling you, it was pleasing to be greeted so warmly. I hadn't considered what it might be like to be the person everyone wanted to impress. It felt good.

"Morning, Peony," Elizabeth said. "How glad I am it's you. Welcome to my home."

Secretly, I imagined that Elizabeth had been angling for the vicar, as I knew how she liked to ingratiate herself with the church community, but I smiled and told her how happy I was to be invited and that I was looking forward to seeing her garden. "You're my very first visit," I said. "Be gentle!"

Elizabeth chuckled. "I will. And the pleasure is all mine."

I followed Elizabeth through a dimly lit hallway decorated with black and white photographs. The faces were so similar to her own that I immediately knew she had a large extended family. A sudden jolt shot through my chest like lightning, and I felt a deep sense of longing wash over me. Was Elizabeth missing someone in particular?

As we emerged into a pretty kitchen at the back of the cottage, I asked Elizabeth about the photographs. Her body stiffened for a moment and then she took hold of herself.

"I have a big family. Three daughters. But they all live in different countries. I miss them terribly. Especially the grandchildren. Why, they grow so fast in-between visits, and I don't have much luck with video chats. Never get the phone to do what it's supposed to do."

I felt terrible for Elizabeth. I knew she was divorced, but I hadn't given much thought to the rest of her family. "That must be hard. But if you'd like, I can help you set up a good video call with your daughters one day. You just let me know when and I'll pop by. You're only a stone's throw from my shop."

Elizabeth smiled broadly and thanked me. I felt a genuine warmth flow through me. Elizabeth had great kindness in her —something which I'd maybe overlooked in the past when she'd been in competition with her old neighbor, Dolores. I was hoping that competitive nature had died down since her friend's passing. I couldn't deal with a week of 'humble bragging', and I was hopeful that Elizabeth's would be an easy first garden to judge.

There was a delicious smell of baking in the air and then I spied a plate with yummy-looking treats.

"Shortbread?" She thrust the plate under my nose.

"Freshly baked this morning. They're still warm. Go on, take one. I've a pot of hibiscus tea as well. Brewed from my own flowers."

I happily accepted a shortbread. I should have known Elizabeth would bake something for my arrival. She had a long-standing reputation in the village of baking to impress, and I wasn't about to complain.

"Delicious," I said, biting into the flaky biscuit.

Elizabeth beamed and poured me a cup of fragrant tea. "Let me take you through to the garden."

After refusing another shortbread, I followed her through to the garden.

It was very pretty indeed. The lawns were freshly mowed, grades of green in neat stripes. My eyes were instantly drawn to her hollyhocks, which were spectacular. Her garden also featured mature roses interspersed with lavender.

"This is just the initial visit," I explained, setting my cup on a windowsill, "and then the shortlisted gardens will all be visited by the full committee later on."

Elizabeth nodded. She hovered close by as I pulled my clipboard and judging chart from my bag.

"I'll just take a look around," I said, hoping Elizabeth would hang back and let me wander freely.

Happily, she took the hint, and I walked through the garden, exploring the verdant beds and careful planting. Despite the recent warm weather, Elizabeth's garden still had a spring-like freshness to it, partly because of the early hour and partly because we'd had recent rain.

A stunning array of evergreens and small silver euca-lyptus trees grew in terracotta pots and up and across the fence which separated her garden from the neighbor's. In a shady spot, jasmine provided glorious scented flowers and glossy green leaves. I could tell that Elizabeth had thought about where the morning and afternoon sun was and which areas might be less hospitable. With my own garden, I liked to think of each section as a room that leads to the next: like a house, a garden should flow. Elizabeth's cottage garden was more playful, less structured than my own, but this imbued the space with an old-world charm I found hard to resist.

I jotted down a few notes before realizing Elizabeth was beside me again. I smiled, understanding how anxious it must be to feel judged on something you had poured your heart and soul into. Although she *had* literally put herself forward for the experience.

"What is it that you enjoy most about your garden?" I asked, reading off Arthur's sheet.

Her eyes glowed and then she paused pensively for a moment before explaining, "It's the sense of accomplishment. I don't mind the boring jobs. Why, I'm just as happy dead-heading the roses as I am when planting something new. I also love to pick flowers from the garden and think it's really wonderful to bring a few little bunches inside on a Friday afternoon. There's nothing so nice in the kitchen as a bouquet of homegrown flowers."

Elizabeth suddenly clapped her hands over her mouth. "I mean, of course, nothing compares to your special bouquets, Peony..."

She trailed off, aghast.

I waved her apology away, laughing. "Don't worry, I won't penalize you for insulting my profession," I joked. "I enjoy flowers from my own garden, too." But as Elizabeth paled, I realized my joke had been in poor taste. I glanced around, looking for a distraction.

"Oh, and aren't those just simply charming," I said, spying her needlework cushions on the outdoor furniture. Elizabeth was a fine needleworker and led the weekly classes run by the Women's Institute at the church hall. "Your handiwork, I take it."

Elizabeth nodded. "Oh yes, hours they took, but worth it, I think. Take a closer look. Each one has a different flower embroidered on the cream linen. Not easy to keep clean but with only me here, it isn't so bad. I hide them from the grand-kids when they do visit."

I smiled and turned a plump cushion in my hands, thinking how nice they'd look in my own garden. Maybe when the competition was over, I could commission Eliza-beth for a few cushions.

With another walk around the garden's circumference, I added some more details to my chart. Without a doubt, the stars of the show were Elizabeth's hollyhocks and her delphiniums with their velvety, deep-blue flowers. I took a few photographs and bid Elizabeth a nice day.

She stood on the curb and waved as I drove off.

CHAPTER 8

*N*ext on my list was Colleen O'Brien's place. It was a short drive away, and I welcomed the breeze as I zipped through the roads with the windows down. The village really was picturesque. It was like driving through a postcard. Although I was tired, I was never too tired not to appreciate the beauty of Willow Waters. It grounded me when all else went haywire 'round here. Which was more often than I would have liked. I was hoping things would calm down after the garden competition ended.

Maybe Alex and I could escape somewhere for a weekend. Dorset or Devon, somewhere by the coast. I was longing to dip my body in the ocean, feel sand between my toes. Maybe it was too soon to be thinking about us going away, but something told me it would be just the tonic once the tourism season ended in the village.

I turned my thoughts back to the competition. I had a feeling Elizabeth's garden would be the most modest of all those on my list. I don't mind telling you that I was intrigued to see Colleen's home. I had no doubts that her garden would be exquisite—her brag book had already proved that—but were her flowers worthy of my shop floor? And could a woman who had supposedly killed a tree over a spat with neighbors be someone I could ever consider working with?

Again, it struck me how strange it was that everyone had an opinion on Colleen O'Brien—some full of praise, others clouded with suspicion. It seemed risky befriending a divisive character when it came to business. It was a small village, and I didn't want to alienate any of my customers. But I agreed with Colleen that more locally-grown flowers would be a nice extra touch for the shop. I would give her a fair chance—it's the least anyone deserved.

I pulled into her road and found a parking space. The morning was getting warmer, the sun baking the asphalt, and I rolled up my three-quarter sleeves as I made my way to Colleen's cottage.

Colleen took less than ten seconds to open the door once I'd rapped on its pretty brass ring knocker with a four-leafed clover for a handle. Unlike yesterday, when Colleen had visited the shop in casual jeans, today she was photograph-ready in a cream dress and had swept back her short red hair with a green headband. She greeted me with a formal hand-shake, as if we were already business partners. The woman was nothing if not confident.

"I've been looking forward to this all morning," she said, ushering me indoors. "Though I'll admit, a touch of the nerves has got to me. Every year, I wonder if I've done enough, done my best. You know how it is when self-doubt sets in. And how nice it's you, Peony, for the first visit."

"Randomly assigned," I admitted, "but I am happy to be here. You have a lovely home." I wasn't lying.

Colleen's cottage was much larger than Elizabeth's, with high ceilings and big windows. The parquet floors and the furniture shone with polish. The air was scented with the remnants of pine cleaner, and a bouquet of freesias was proudly displayed on the hallway sideboard. I noted them silently, the perfect bell-shaped blooms on each stem, the sweetness of their fragrance. Had she grown them? Perhaps she owned a greenhouse. I was impressed.

"Can I get you some proper Irish tea?" Colleen asked, ushering me into a tidy kitchen. "And I've made fresh soda bread. It's my grandmother's recipe."

I thanked Colleen but refused the offer. I couldn't be eating cake and biscuits at every house—although it *was* tempting.

But she looked so downcast, I relented. "Oh, go on," I said. Perhaps I could call this an early lunch.

"We'll have it outside," she said, gathering a tray that was already prepared. All she had to do was boil the kettle. She made the tea in that Irish china with a cream background and tiny green shamrocks all over it. Belleek? Was that the name?

As I looked at her, it crossed my mind that she'd dressed to match her china. No, I thought. She couldn't be that calculating. Could she?

Four slices of soda bread were displayed on a plate in the same china, and we had individual tea plates, cups, and saucers, and crisply-ironed linen napkins. She placed it all on a tray and led the way through a side door in her kitchen that opened to the garden.

Colleen chattered on about the warm weather, no hint of nerves at the impending judging or potential business deal despite her initial confession of self-doubt. We emerged into a short alley, where the brick trailed with sumptuous ivy, and rounded the corner to the garden.

I couldn't help it: I gasped at the sight. In real life, Colleen's garden was picture-perfect. Absolutely immaculate. Covering about two hundred square feet, the garden sprang up around a gushing water fountain centerpiece. Every bloom, every bed, was weedless and neatly edged. It was almost too perfect, yet I couldn't fault the incredible artistry.

I was immediately drawn to Colleen's famous reblooming irises, whose flaming orange color was heightened by the gold of the sun. In fact, the whole of the garden was dazzling with color, shades of red, orange, and yellow complementing one another and cleverly recurring in different blooms through the beds, drawing the eye through the landscape and providing both a focal point and a cohesive feel. I knew that using bold, brighter hues was also perfect for directing attention away from objects you'd prefer not to view, and a particularly bright patch was planted by a sunny spot right beside the garden fence where I figured her neighbors' once-towering tree had stood. I frowned at the sight, hoping it really was all just a silly misunderstanding between the two households. Bad communication between neighbors could lead to some terrible and unnecessary fallings-out.

I noticed a few small figures standing on rocks or hiding amongst the flowers. The famous garden gnomes.

We sat at a round, wrought-iron table strategically located to enjoy the garden views. The scents of rose and honeysuckle drifted by, then I caught a hint of geranium.

"I so wish Gabriel was here to meet you as well," Colleen said as we sipped tea and nibbled on soda bread.

The soda bread was excellent, by the way, slightly sweet and studded with raisins, and thickly spread with butter.

"It's so hard on him being back in Ireland looking after his ma. But, as he says, she raised him to be the kind of man who does right by his family. You can't ask for a better man." She blinked quickly, and I realized how much she must miss him.

"And so you do all the gardening yourself?" I asked.

"I have to while my husband's gone. But I don't mind. It keeps me strong and fills my days. And I always feel like Gabriel's with me when I'm in the garden we built together."

I left the table and walked around, taking notes and photographs, noting the shamrocks with a smile and how Colleen was quite literally bringing her Irish roots to the Cotswold soil. And it was a pleasant surprise to see just how many gnomes she owned. I counted eight in total, each one unique and gorgeous. They looked similar to my Yasmin, and I asked her if they were from Woolfeder Gnomes.

Colleen looked impressed. "Indeed. You've got a good eye, Peony. And good taste. I simply can't abide all the nonsense plastic rubbish out there. I've been collecting *proper* gnomes this year." She swept her hand around the garden. "This isn't my full collection. I swap them out according to seasons and colors and what's in bloom." Then she tsked. "What are you doing over there?" She addressed a bearded gnome sitting on a barrel playing a flute.

He wore a red pointed hat, a yellow jacket, and gray baggy trousers. He seemed to be playing to a female gnome who sat on a swing, gazing off into the distance.

Colleen grabbed the flute player by his barrel and set him in a patch of yellow marguerites. "There," she said. "That's better. The yellow of his jacket and the yellow of the flowers match, you see. A winning garden is about attention to the tiniest detail."

Secretly, I wondered how Colleen could afford to buy so many Woolfeder Gnomes. I'd seen the catalog, and I knew they came with a hefty price tag. Colleen and her husband were retired, and pension checks could only go so far. Maybe they had savings she was dipping into. And why not? If you can't enjoy life's little luxuries when you're retired, when can you?

She took my arm like we were old friends and walked me over to where a gnome with a wheelbarrow and another with a pair of shears were perched prettily next to the white freesias I'd admired inside. "Take these two, for example," she said. "They're my latest additions. The one with the wheelbarrow is Marc, the other Patrick. The creaminess of their complexion perfectly matches the freesias. No accident."

We strolled to her patch of vibrant shamrocks where a gnome was carrying a basket. "This cheeky chappy isn't German. He's English, and you can tell from the complexion. No alpine goat's milk for him, I'm afraid. But I find his rosy cheeks and red basket offset the green of the shamrocks."

I conceded that Colleen had an eye for color and her blooms were of great quality, all the while clapping myself on the back for being open to stocking gnomes. More and more, I was determined to give them a go—even if Imogen didn't approve. At least I'd have one good customer in Colleen.

I continued my tour and ended by the water fountain centerpiece, which featured a stone statue of an angel. It was set off from the rest of the garden, resting on a circle of gravel.

"The birds like to have a bath in my fountain," she said. "I do love to watch them. I saw the statue in the garden center and bought it immediately. It wasn't cheap, mind you, but it makes me smile every day. Still, it's backbreaking work without my husband to help."

"Do you manage to get over there?" I asked. "To Ireland, I mean?"

"As often as I can," Colleen replied. "But short-haul flights aren't so cheap anymore. It all adds up. We're hoping he can be back home for good by Christmas."

I asked her the question I'd asked Elizabeth. "What is it that you enjoy most about your garden?"

She glanced around as though she'd never seen her garden before. "I suppose it's the sense of accomplishment. I look at my garden as though it were an artist's canvas. Every year I paint a different picture." And didn't that sound like the perfect sound bite for her acceptance speech when she won?

Then, before my eyes, her pensive expression turned sour. She sniffed the air. Once, twice, a third time, like a dog sniffing the breeze, before wrinkling her nose in disgust. "How dare they?" she muttered, her fury obvious even though she kept her tone low. "I can't believe they're doing this to me. Again. Today of all days. Wicked. That's what it is. Wicked."

Now the scent had reached me, too. A smell that reminded me of the Fourth of July back home. I was suddenly nostalgic for hamburgers on the grill, watermelon, iced tea, and fireworks.

She shook her head. "That awful stench. Can't you smell it? Stinking up the air with a barbecue. And who barbecues so early in the morning? It's a ploy, I tell you. A ploy."

I didn't admit how much I liked the smell, though it definitely dampened my ability to enjoy the scents of Colleen's garden.

Then the sound of some experimental jazz sprang up. This was less pleasing.

I couldn't help but wince at the discordant trombones. "Are your neighbors jazz enthusiasts?" I asked. I had to speak up over the racket.

But she paid my question no attention. "I can't believe them," Colleen said, pacing now in fury. "They must have seen you arrive and devised a way of ruining my chances in the garden competition by spoiling the atmosphere. No doubt they've been sitting up at night, planning this for weeks."

I laughed. Surely Colleen wasn't being serious? But her mouth was set and her eyes glittered. She was deadly serious.

"It has no bearing on the judging," I assured her. "A little charcoal and some music won't affect your score. Besides, I've got everything I need. My visit is coming to an end." I gave Colleen a reassuring broad smile. "And if they meant to ruin any ambience, they'll suffer, too. Their garden is the next on my list."

Colleen did not look consoled. "Well, I'm sorry for you that you're about to waste your time. I'm sure they've only entered the competition to spite me. There's nothing in that wasteland but a few rocks and some moss. Ghastly." She shook her head again. "They're from *London*, you know," she said, like the city was a dirty word. "Always going back and forth. Piling into their Prius with a mountain of suitcases, making an awful disturbance. But when they are actually here, it's like they're set on ruining the village. If I had my way, they'd be uprooted like the weeds they are."

I was taken aback by Colleen's venom. A little summer BBQ and some jazz was hardly fodder for such a take-down. Neither was loading suitcases into a Prius. A cold feeling came over me. Now that I had been exposed to the spite Imogen had warned me about, it was easy to believe Colleen had indeed killed her neighbors' ancient tree on purpose. It was like a light had flicked off in her and something dark had been allowed to take over.

I was having second thoughts about the idea of working with Colleen, despite her lovely blooms. Thankfully, she was too immersed in the judging experience, and her disproportionate annoyance, to bring up the subject of business. I was glad.

Suddenly, a mower started up next door, its roar loud and grating and not harmonizing at all with the jazz. I began to suspect that Colleen wasn't being completely unreasonable. It did seem like her neighbors were deliberately ruining the peace of the morning.

"I'd like to get my hands on them," Colleen snapped.

But I wasn't about to take the conversation any further. I thanked her for her time, told her we'd be in touch, and felt a little relieved as I left her house. Emotions in the village were certainly running high.

I walked around her cottage down the narrow path and once in the front, I spotted Marty, the new village postman, on his rounds. He waved and then crossed the street to say hello.

"What a coincidence," he said. "I suppose you're here for the garden competition?"

I nodded, not wanting to get into it any further. I was sure that one wrong word taken out of context would send a flurry of rumors through the village.

"I was just heading to Colleen's," he said, as if they were old friends. He nodded to a postcard in his hand sitting atop an envelope.

I could see that the postcard was from Ireland. *Greetings from Galway*, it said, and there was a scene of the Irish countryside.

Marty turned the postcard over. A few lines were written in a hasty scrawl. Gabriel was probably too busy to write much more, but it was romantic that he was making the effort to write.

"It's sad when people live far apart from their loved ones," he said, "but at least the post keeps them connected."

I nodded. Marty was right. I hadn't given much thought to the post as a way to still connect. We were all so used to phones and video calls and emails nowadays. But I could see the attraction in a handwritten note. Even if it was a short one.

Then he tapped the envelope. "Love and pension checks keep the heart beating and the lights burning."

And now I saw that it was some kind of government envelope.

He dipped his head in goodbye and strolled up to Colleen's front door, leaving me reeling. Our new postman was so indiscreet. He seemed to spend as much time checking out the mail we received as delivering it.

I resolved then and there never to have anything personal sent to the farmhouse—not unless I wanted the whole of Willow Waters to know about it.

CHAPTER 9

I braced myself before ringing the bell on the smart red door of Colleen's neighboring cottage. Who was waiting for me on the other side? A snobby couple from London, intent on ruining Colleen's pleasure? Or two mild-mannered people with a fondness for barbecued chicken, a penchant for experimental jazz, and a sudden urge to mow the lawn while listening to that jazz?

Hopefully the latter, although the way my morning had developed, I hoped it wouldn't end in a screaming match over the fence. The last thing I wanted was to play mediator.

The second I rang the bell, the lawn mower stopped. And then the bleating jazz, which I could hear even from the street, abruptly ended. I smiled to myself. Coincidence? Or was all that palaver only designed to upset Colleen? Her neighbors certainly knew how to press the right buttons.

Unlike my first two visits, it took quite some time before the door opened. I watched Marty as he made his rounds down the street. Friendly but nosy. Not the greatest combination. But thoughts of Marty disappeared as a deep voice said,

"Good morning," and I turned back to the house to see a very tall man smiling down at me, while he stood in the now open doorway.

"Hi," I said. And introduced myself and the reason for my visit.

"Greg Lawley," he said, extending his hand and shaking mine firmly. "We've been expecting you. My wife and I are so excited for your visit." He flashed a set of pearly teeth, bright against the deep tan of his face.

He stepped outside, closed the front door behind him, and led me along a side alley to the garden. I was somewhat relieved not to be invited into another kitchen and plied with more sweets. Thankfully, he was eager to get me to the garden.

"We have all kinds of treats waiting for you, Peony," he said. "My wife, Erica, has made some of her famous iced tea, and she's been cooking up a storm. I do so hope you like matcha—we're quite obsessed with it in this household, and Erica makes the most fabulous matcha and white chocolate chip cookies."

So much for not being plied with sweets.

Inwardly, I groaned, thinking of my impending dental bills and expanding waistline. Then the sound of classical musical started up. I recognized the uplifting violin of Vivaldi's Spring. I smiled. You didn't need a witch's intuition to see these two were playing *me* as well as Colleen. But I was here to judge their garden—not winning personalities.

After Colleen's spiteful words, I'd been preparing to be underwhelmed by her neighbors' garden, but as we stepped into the sunlight again, I was truly blown away. In front of me was a serene zen garden. Although small, it was immaculate, peaceful, and minimalist. I'd never seen anything like it. Evergreens stole the show, in a wild variety of heights, sizes, and interesting textures. There was almost no color apart from an odd splash of white and vivid red. To say it was a contrast to Colleen's was an understatement.

Greg stood beside me as I took it all in. He obviously enjoyed my surprise. "I'm extremely proud of our little meditation garden," he said. "We've worked very hard. I think it's paid off. But you're the official judge of that." He laughed nervously. Although twice the size of Colleen, he had none of her bluster. In fact, he struck me as more of an introvert. There was something mellow about Greg. Whether it was the garden's influence or he imbued the garden with his own spirit, it was quite lovely to see.

"It's beautiful," I conceded. "No two ways about it. And very unique for these parts."

To the right of the garden was a Japanese maple reflecting its fire-like gold and orange leaves across a pond. It looked like a poem.

Greg nodded. "We think so, too. We wanted to be inspired by the principles we live our lives by. The Japanese garden is a process of distillation and serenity, so overcrowding your space just for the sake of it is a huge *faux pas* in Japanese culture."

He explained that they'd tried to follow the Japanese concept of *Ma,* which was about creating the sense of balance that has both movement and stillness. "The garden should be filled with nothing but energy and feeling," he concluded.

We walked 'round slowly. There was a space dedicated to a dry garden with no plants at all, just sand, gravel, and granite. A rake had been used to create patterns in the sand and the result was calming, like watching waves gently roll against a beach. The position of stones and boulders added another, more natural element. It was wonderful. But I could see why Colleen found the whole thing a joke. It couldn't be further from her style of garden. Personally, I found it refreshing.

"Our garden was designed with peacefulness and meditation in mind," a woman's voice said. I turned, and there was Erica, Greg's wife. She was holding a bronze tray with a pitcher of iced tea and the aforementioned matcha and white chocolate chip cookies on it. "Welcome," she added, "we're so happy to receive you."

Erica was captivating. Roughly half her husband's height, she was wearing a blue cotton dress which came down to her feet and made her look like she was floating. Her skin was luminous, offset by the shiny, billowing black hair which fell down her back. Her dark eyes twinkled as she insisted I take a biscuit.

There was no point protesting. I bit into the pale-green cookie, delighted by its soft, gooey texture. The sweetness of the white chocolate was a perfect match for the bitterness of the matcha. I thanked Erica and told her how much I liked her garden.

She set the tray on a cast-iron table and then explained they'd been inspired by a zen garden in London's Holland Park. "It was built in celebration of London's Japan Festival as a symbol of friendship between our two countries," she said. "Of course, we can't compare to something in Holland Park. That part of the city is uber pricey. But we took note of its super-traditional design, the amazing tranquil waterfalls, and more calming bodies of water. There is even a shoal of koi carp. Obviously, we couldn't do anything on the same scale here, but the pond *has* been our labor of love." She smiled pleasantly. "Go take a closer look if you like."

I followed Erica to the pond. It was modest in size, around eight feet long, but was cleverly planted with floating waterlilies and a water hyacinth. Eelgrass licked the sides. It was then I saw two koi carp flick their tails.

"Wow," I whispered as the fish maneuvered their strong bodies through the greenish water. Then I asked the question I'd asked Elizabeth and Colleen. "What is it that you enjoy most about your garden?"

Erica sighed happily. "I find myself coming out here first thing in the morning with a cup of matcha and just being quiet for ten minutes before the day starts. It's especially relaxing in the moments after the sun rises. I enjoy the peace." She lifted her gaze from the pond and turned toward the fence. Her whole demeanor suddenly shifted. Shoulders rounded, her body tensed as if preparing itself for an attack.

Peace was not her uppermost emotion.

"If it wasn't for *her* next door. The minute she sees me out here meditating, she starts bashing her gardening tools and playing her radio at full blast. Some dreadful chat program. Without her, this would be the most peaceful spot on earth," she added.

Great, just what I needed—another snide remark from the other side of the fence. I decided not to take the bait. I had to remain impartial, above the fray.

I strolled around, making notes and taking photos while Erica and Greg sat at the garden table. They whispered, seemingly embroiled in a frantic exchange. I assumed it was just nerves and got on with my job.

When I'd completed a full circle, I made my way back to the couple. Both were frowning, but smoothed their expression as I joined them.

Greg, however, retained some nervous energy. His knee juddered up and down, and he placed one hand on his thigh to steady it. "Sorry if my wife sounded unkind. We may come across as intense, but the garden means a lot to us. A real labor of love. And research. Sadly, we had to redo a section of it, because that evil witch next door killed our beautiful sycamore tree."

My back prickled. There was nothing I disliked more than someone using the word witch as a curse word. Greg should be careful with his language. I felt my cheeks redden, but took a deep breath.

"Witch is not the right word," I said carefully, "but I did hear something about your tree," I admitted.

"We're hoping to plant a new one," Greg said. "White-beam round two. In a different spot, of course."

But Erica's reaction was much more embittered. She crinkled her nose and said, "I bet you've only heard *her* version of the story. Where we're the terrible out-of-towners who moved to *her* village and continued to ruin *her* precious sunspot."

Greg shot his wife a warning look, but it was ignored.

She said, "Shortly after we moved here, Colleen asked us to cut down the tree because the shade was affecting her garden. She claimed the previous owners had promised to do it, but then moved before they got around to it. We actually asked the previous owners, and they said they'd absolutely refused to cut down the tree. They didn't say so, but we got the idea they moved because Colleen was such an unpleasant neighbor."

"A tree is a living thing, after all," Greg said, "far older and grander than we are."

"Plus, we liked the shade and privacy," Erica added. "But she wouldn't listen. Was so insistent. Day after day, the moaning, the beseeching. Eventually, we fell out and stopped speaking to one another. She waited until we went on holiday. A few weeks in India, and when we came back, the tree had mysteriously died. We had to cut the whole thing down." Erica shook her head. "It was a tragedy."

"Colleen tried to say it was afflicted by some tree disease," Greg added, scoffing. "Absolute nonsense. But we could never prove it was her."

Erica narrowed her eyes and lowered her voice. "I've looked into it," she said, fixing me with her intense gaze. "I think she used something called the 'hack and squirt method.'"

I must have looked puzzled because she explained this method used a small axe to tear away part of the bark of the tree to sneakily insert a herbicide into the trunk.

"We wanted to sue her," Erica continued, "but Daddy said there wasn't enough evidence, so we'd be better not to bother."

Greg sighed. "And Daddy knows everything," he said in a tone that had more than a hint of a sneer.

Erica immediately bridled. "He knows about this. Daddy is a high court judge. He's an authority on the law."

"He's also the man who tried to convince you not to marry me." Greg turned and addressed me directly. "Said she was marrying down. Right in front of me. It's one of the reasons we moved here. I've never had the kind of job or made the kind of money that would impress Erica's family. We could never afford in London what we've been able to buy in this village. The city priced us out." Greg paused and then added quickly, "Not that we don't love it here. We do. We're Willowers through and through."

Again, I wanted to tell this couple I wasn't here to judge their personalities. Working in retail had taught me the art of discretion.

Erica shrugged. They had obviously had this conversation a hundred times. If not more. "We're from different worlds." She turned from her husband to face me squarely and then proceeded to talk as if he wasn't there. "We met at the spa where I work as a receptionist. He came in for a meditation class and a massage. We got to talking, and the rest is history. Making this a meditation garden reminds us both of how we met. Mummy and Daddy were very disappointed, of course, but I feel that if we win this competition, they'll see that we haven't failed. We're doing really well for ourselves without their help."

I tried to keep my face neutral. Yet again, I'd been sucked into the personal lives of the competition participants. Alex had warned me how seriously people took this contest, but I hadn't realized it would be so...intimate. I was learning as much about people's personal lives as their gardens. It was unnerving. I had to get this conversation back to the garden.

So I asked who did most of the gardening, and Greg replied that it was mostly his wife. "I commute to Cheltenham for work. Erica has the time."

A breeze blew across the garden and the pretty sound of wind chimes followed. I glanced around and noticed that there were also crystals placed along the windowsills. I was sure they had been bought from my mom's shop.

Erica followed my gaze. "That's all Greg," she said. "He's the one who's into meditation and all that. And the Buddhas." She pointed at three squat Buddha statues. They were a far cry from Colleen's gnomes; I could see why the neighbors clashed so often.

Greg frowned at his wife. "You could use some more meditation. Might show you there's more to life than status."

I swallowed. I didn't think Erica had meant anything bad by her comment. Maybe Greg needed to work on his own meditation practice a bit more. Perhaps a quick temper had caused him to turn to the practice in the first place.

Erica shot daggers at her husband and then cleared her throat. "Won't you have some iced tea, Peony?"

I accepted a glass, pretty thirsty after all the tension. I'd placed my clipboard face down on the table, and I noticed Erica eyeing it now. Next to the clipboard was a pile of mail that Marty must have just delivered. An open envelope had a flyer beside it—the words UNPLUG in gold caught my eye. From a brief glance, I could tell it was about a silent meditation retreat, but then I caught myself—did I want to be as nosy as Marty?

Erica also noticed the flyer. "Sorry about the mess," she said, picking it up. She restacked the unopened letters and then made a move to scrunch the flyer but Greg's hand shot out.

"Don't," he said. "I might want to go. I *am* seeking enlightenment, after all."

Erica laughed, a harsh sound which made me instantly uncomfortable. "You're not so enlightened that you don't want to take the old bat next door down a notch."

But at this comment, Greg visibly relaxed. "You're right,"

he said, smiling again. To me, he said, "I'm afraid our little feud made us even more determined to outdo Colleen's garden. No better way to get at her than to take away her beloved best-garden trophy."

I remained silent. What a troubled couple, caught up in pettiness while also seeking enlightenment.

But I had to admit, they did have a very nice garden.

CHAPTER 10

After a morning brimming with other people's nerves and tension, it was a relief to pull up outside my beloved Bewitching Blooms. Honestly, the last two hours had felt more like a year. After running my own business single-handedly until Imogen came along, I thought I knew the meaning of hard work.

I'd never subscribed to Sartre's statement that 'Hell is other people.' I thrived on working in the community, getting to know my customers and all their little foibles. I loved stopping to converse with a neighbor on the street or making pleasant chit-chat at Roberto's. But now I could see a bit more of Sartre's point. Certain other people, if not hell, were definitely draining.

As an antidote, I figured I'd turn my attention to the little versions of us—to gnomes, I mean. After talking with Bernard, hearing about Marty's deliveries, and seeing Colleen's impressive collection, I planned to call Thomas Woolfe this afternoon and place an order from his glossy catalog. It would have to be small. I couldn't afford to take risks, but I was willing to give the gnomes a try. Something was telling me to trust my instincts. And you know by now that a witch never ignores her instincts.

Unbuckling my seatbelt, I reached in the back of my Range Rover for Yasmin, the gnome, to return her to the prime position by the till. But to my surprise, she wasn't there!

I figured I must have been driving faster than I thought. Desperate to get away from Tension Alley.

I turned, wriggling in my seat to see where she'd fallen, but no. Nothing. Just an old hard-candy wrapper and a parrot treat.

"How strange," I murmured. I was convinced I'd brought Yasmin with me this morning to continue trialing her appeal at the shop. I remembered having the thought in the garden. I wasn't usually so forgetful. Maybe the competition had got the better of me and I'd become distracted.

Now I thought about it... I hadn't locked my Range Rover this morning. Not outside the rectory and not at either of my garden visits. But this was Willow Waters, where I knew my neighbors and people looked out for each other. However, it was also a tourist town, and who knew how many light-fingered strangers might have passed my vehicle and been tempted by Yasmin?

But I didn't like that theory. Was it possible Yasmin could have fallen out somehow? Had I opened the back doors at any point in my visits? I closed my eyes for a moment, trying to remember. I didn't think that had happened.

Which took me back to the scenario where an oppor-tunist had seen her sitting there, looking so pretty in the back of my car, and walked off with the gnome.

Perplexed, I breathed a sigh of relief when I looked across the sidewalk and saw Imogen's serene face behind Bewitching Blooms' counter. Nothing ever ruffled Imogen. No rude customer or bizarre request. I felt calmer just watching her.

I got out of the car, remembering to lock it this time, and entered my shop, happy to be back in my natural habitat.

And to add to my happiness, Yasmin was beside the till. "Oh, am I happy to see you," I said to the gnome. I must have left her at the farmhouse after all, and Char had brought her back to the shop. Happy to have that mystery solved, I turned to ask Imogen how things had been in my absence.

"I have to give you credit for knowing your customers better than I do," she said. "We've had so many comments on the gnome and three orders."

"That's great," I said, pleased for myself but also happy to support a local artisanal business. I patted Yasmin's head as though she were a good-luck charm.

Imogen reported that sales had been reasonable for a Saturday. Char had operated the till while she'd worked with flowers, but when it got quiet, Char said she'd go tinker with Frodo if she wasn't needed. I had a feeling Char was trying to get the engine to turn on by magic.

Then Imogen turned to me with a sly grin and asked in a too-innocent voice, "How did it all go this morning?"

"I think you already know the answer," I replied with a sigh, settling behind the computer to check the morning's sales. "Exhausting."

"Well, don't say I didn't warn you," she said. "Shall I get us a treat from Roberto's and you can tell me everything?"

I shuddered at the idea of one more sweet treat, then

told her how I'd been bribed with sugar at every stop. "It's even more difficult than I'd imagined. Everyone is so competitive and emotional, and each garden was lovely in its own way. It seems unfair to compare. I wish we'd split the prizes into different categories so we could put more people through the shortlist, but Arthur insisted it was too much work."

Imogen laughed at me. "Peony, you're going to have to toughen up. Every competition has winners and losers. It's the name of the game."

Imogen was right. One of the drawbacks of a witch's deep intuition was a tendency to be oversensitive, a sponge for others' pain. But something about the morning lingered in my being. It wasn't just the disproportionate sense of competition between the contestants. An undercurrent of dread rippled through me.

I DECIDED to put the competition out of mind for now when Justine Johnson walked in. She looked as worn out by the morning as I knew I did. We shared conspiratorial looks as Imogen said hello and asked Justine if she had enjoyed her first judging experience.

Justine laughed in her light way, her brown bob bouncing. "Let's just say it provided a new insight into village life."

"An introduction to its sordid underbelly?" I joked.

Justine puffed out her cheeks and blew out her breath. "More like its *actual* belly. Every stop involved a cup of tea or coffee and some homemade delight. By the end, I was completely stuffed. But their poor faces when I tried to decline a biscuit. It was like I'd just told them their beloved pet had died. I didn't have it in me to refuse."

"Tell me about it," I moaned. "They're trying to bribe us with cake and tea."

"And I'm afraid it's working," Justine said. "I'll be impartial, of course. That goes with the day job. But I am especially fond of shortbread, and everyone seems to know about it."

I laughed. Out of earshot from Imogen, we exchanged notes and photographs from our mornings. If I thought a problem shared was a problem halved, then this competition proved the exception to the rule. Each garden was full of charm, so disparate from one another and all the better for it. It was very confusing. And this was only a small percentage of the qualifying gardens. How we would ever make a decision was beyond me.

The phone rang, and since Imogen was busy with a new customer looking for the perfect scented candle, Justine said her goodbyes and I was happy to return to my actual job.

"Good afternoon, Bewitching Blooms," I said. "Peony speaking, how can I help?"

A honey-like voice filled my ears. It belonged to Gillian Fairfax, the glamorous and recently widowed ex-model who lived at the historic Lemmington House at the top of a hill at the north end of the village. I hadn't always seen eye-to-eye with Gillian (she was a flamboyant flirt and downright snobby) but over the past few months, I'd seen a softer, more vulnerable side to Gillian. Even if I still thoroughly disapproved of her choice in men.

"I'm glad it's you, Peony," Gillian said. "You always know exactly what I want, even when I can't describe it."

I glowed at the compliment. It's what I hope for with all

my clients—delivering the vision they didn't even know they'd had. She went on to explain that she had invited a few locals to Sunday lunch the next day and was after a stunning but understated bouquet. "Peregrine Fygg-Burton, his wife Lottie, and the Wilkinsons are coming." She dropped the names so I'd understand how socially important this lunch was.

The Fygg-Burtons had a large house on the river and the Wilkinsons owned the Tudor Rose, the best hotel and restaurant in town. As Gillian tried to climb back up the social ladder, since pretty much tumbling to the bottom, I knew she'd want every detail of her lunch to be perfect.

One of Gillian's favorite things was to provide me with oxymorons when it came to her design briefs. Or worse, give no guidance at all. Stunning but understated? Really?

"On it," I said and asked for a budget and desired size.

"A hundred and fifty," Gillian answered breezily. "Sorry for the late notice. But the sooner you can get it over, the better." She paused. "And maybe include something pale pink. I have a new silk dress and lipstick I'd like to coordinate with."

Of *course* Gillian wanted flowers to match her outfit. I told her no problem and that I'd drop the arrangement at Lemmington House on my way home that evening. Gillian breathed a sigh of relief, thanked me, and said she'd see me later.

I probably wouldn't have offered every customer such great service, but Gillian was wealthy, and when she bought flowers, she didn't stint. I knew she'd appreciate it if I made the effort to deliver at short notice. Especially if I made the call personally. What Gillian didn't need to know was that my last judging stop of the day was to Vera Brown's. Since the two houses were pretty close, I wouldn't even be going out of my way.

I took a deep breath at the thought of visiting another garden. I could only hope that Vera would prove to be more relaxed than my other entrants.

While Imogen rang up the two scented candles she'd managed to convince our customer to buy, I dug out the Woolfeder Gnomes catalog. If we'd already pre-sold three Yasmins, I should stock a few more styles. Flicking through, I spotted some of Colleen's collection. And then their prices. The gnomes she'd chosen were both charming and expensive. If Colleen had that amount of cash to spend on gnomes, then so might other villagers and visitors.

After much deliberation, I chose models with broad appeal and differing price tags and called the number listed on in the catalog.

After a few rings, Thomas Woolfe picked up the phone himself.

I smiled down the line at his softly spoken voice and told him that I'd decided to give the gnomes a go in my shop.

He didn't seem a bit surprised that we'd already pre-sold three. "I had a feeling your shop would be a good home for the little creatures."

As the shopping day drew toward closing time, I looked forward to a Saturday night with my feet up, recovering from the day's garden judging.

Imogen told me she had a date. Not that she'd needed to inform me. I could tell from her air of suppressed excitement and the way she kept glancing at her phone.

I wished her good luck and silently admired her resilience. She was a serial first dater.

"Thanks, Peony," she said. "I have a good feeling about this one."

"I hope he deserves you."

Imogen looked at me from under her lashes. "I hope so too."

I didn't know why, but Imogen could never seem to get past date two with anyone—no matter how eligible the bachelor. There was something restless about Imogen when it came to her romantic life. In a way, I admired it. Twenty-four was a beautiful age. Everything ahead of you like an endless school summer holiday. What I didn't miss was knowing myself as well as I did now. And all those awkward first dates. Although maybe I wasn't the one to talk about dating since I'd embarked on my own slow dating relationship with Alex over the last month. I didn't know what the future held for us, but at least I never felt awkward around Alex. A witch and a werewolf—an easy-going match, as it turned out.

I wasn't as well-trained in floristry as Imogen, but I had a knack for creating a bouquet that looked as though the homeowner had just run out to the garden and gathered an armful of perfect blooms and tossed them together. It suited Gillian, as she actually had that kind of garden, just not the time or talent to put it all together.

At four o'clock, I said goodbye to Imogen and left her to close.

I carefully set Gillian's magnificent white and pale-pink bouquet in the back of my car. I had one more stop to make in my role as a garden competition judge, and since the contestants had been asked to stand by between nine and five today, I needed to be there soon. I was looking forward to seeing Vera and her sweet sheep dog Milton. With the latter in mind, I grabbed several liver treats that I kept near the till for visiting dogs. Milton was very partial to them.

The best thing about my last stop in the judging circuit was that there'd be no drama. At least I hoped not. I'd had enough drama for one day.

But little did I know what was ahead.

CHAPTER 11

*S*ince I didn't want the fresh bouquet wilting, I headed to Lemmington House first. It was a pleasant drive to Gillian Fairfax's house. These days, it was unusual for me to be driving alone. Char and Norman were often in the car, so I had time to myself to think about the surprising day I was having.

The village lanes were busy now with weekend traffic, but it was a pleasure to observe the trees and meadows as the rows of cars ebbed forward. I was instantly soothed by being surrounded by nature.

A short while later, I reached Gillian's house to deliver her pink-toned arrangement. It still felt a little strange to be delivering flowers for Gillian rather than her late husband, Alistair, who had loved to spoil his young wife with beautiful bouquets. He'd only died a few months ago, but since then, Gillian had been linked with a string of unsuitable men. She was a beautiful woman, a former model who'd inherited a manor house and a fortune when her much older husband died. Still, she seemed to need a man to feel complete.

So, I wasn't surprised when I turned into her enormous drive to see her shapely silhouette in the distance alongside that of a man I didn't recognize. Gillian always had a man in tow.

Clutching the enormous bouquet, I saw no use in ringing the doorbell and instead walked around the side of the house where the two figures were now sitting opposite one another in a shaded area of grass by a low stone wall.

But as I got closer, I saw that the two figures were sitting cross-legged, in lotus position. Hmm, I didn't take Gillian for the yoga type. Her thing was tennis. Especially her instructor.

The man opposite her had his back to me. Gillian's eyes were closed. I heard him murmur something and their hands reached out to each other, clasping. Then they began to sway back and forth. Her blonde hair was pulled back, and she wore the kind of chic yoga clothes that looked designed to flatter the wearer rather than catch sweat.

Her partner sported a well-worn gray T-shirt and black athletic shorts. There was something familiar about him, and I edged to the side, hoping to see his profile.

My heart sank when I recognized Greg Lawley, Colleen O'Brien's neighbor. And, more to the point, Erica Lawley's husband. I'd sensed trouble between the couple, but surely he wasn't foolish enough to romance a woman in the same village. Was he?

There was something very cozy about the two of them clasping hands and rocking, and I crept back again, planning to leave the flowers at Gillian's front door. I'd barely taken a step back when she opened her eyes. She gave a slight gasp and tugged her hands out of Greg's.

"Peony!" she said sharply.

I don't know why I felt guilty, all I'd done was deliver the flowers she'd ordered, but I found myself stumbling over words as I told her I'd brought her flowers for her lunch tomorrow, which was self-evident since I was holding them.

"Of course," she said, rising gracefully to standing. All that tennis and yoga was definitely keeping her supple.

Perhaps she was hoping I didn't know her companion, but unfortunately we'd met.

He turned and looked as embarrassed as I felt. "Peony, how nice to see you again."

Hah. I was guessing that was a big fat whopper.

"Greg is teaching me to meditate," Gillian said quickly. "It really helps with my anxiety."

"Gillian needs to relax more," he said, as if sensing he needed an excuse for their cozy party of two. "We're working on her entering into a dialogue with her inner child and letting herself be playful."

By the looks of it, Gillian was playful enough for all three of us.

She came toward me and complimented me on my bouquet, which was flattering, but I suspected she was more interested in keeping me friendly. And less likely to gossip.

"I'll put these in water."

"And I should be going," Greg said, getting up from the grass.

I wished them both a pleasant weekend and got back in my car.

"Not your business," I said aloud as I pulled out of Lemmington House.

But I didn't have a good feeling about what I'd seen.

I WAS ACTUALLY LOOKING FORWARD to seeing Vera. I was fairly certain there'd be no drama in her garden, no strange men visiting. She often came into Bewitching Blooms with her beloved dog. Vera was a widow, and Milton was her beloved companion. Like the poet he was named for, poor Milton had gone blind in his old age. Also deaf. But he still had his sense of smell and taste and seemed to enjoy his quiet life.

I knew Vera had a small but pretty garden, but it was her roses which were famous in the village. She rarely bought a bouquet from my shop, but I enjoyed chatting with her when she popped in. Despite her years, Vera was full of life. And now that she had her grandson Neil and his young family living near her, I was certain she'd feel less alone.

On the way to Vera's, I drove past Barnham House, the historical manor with a significant historical dig going on in its extensive gardens. The previous owner had given the property to the village, and after consultation, it had been offered as a rental. I didn't know what the rent was, but part of the deal was that the tenants would keep an eye on the place and they'd have to live with an archaeological dig/TV show going on in their garden.

Neil and his family had been the successful applicants for the tenancy, to everyone's satisfaction. They'd made the move from London and now looked after Vera as well as Barnham House. Neil had a good job in finance in London but was able to work from home part of the week. And who wouldn't face a bit of commuting in order to live in a beautiful home with a fascinating history?

Vera's home was exactly the kind of Cotswold cottage that

ended up on postcards, and no doubt hers had. Made of the honey-colored stone local to the area, the cottage even featured a thatch roof, which I'm very partial to, though I hear they are a nightmare to maintain.

Unlike my other visits today, Vera had a substantial front garden. To my relief, Vera wasn't waiting outside for my arrival in the last minutes before my deadline of 5 p.m. She also didn't immediately open her door when I knocked. I didn't mind. It gave me a moment to catch my breath and admire the gorgeous pink Penny Lane roses, which scrambled over an arch at the end of the path leading to her front door. Traditional in style, with perfect symmetry, the two beds on either side of the path were bursting with recently-clipped shrubs interspersed with hardy and colorful perennials which spilled onto the walkway. Wisteria covered the front of her house, the last of the purple pendants hanging on despite the onset of summer.

I smiled, already charmed.

Eventually, Vera opened the door, full of apologies for the delay. "It's these old legs of mine," she said, shaking her head. "They can't seem to keep up with my commands!"

If Vera had noticed I was close to being late, she was too polite to say anything. She ushered me in and together we walked through a floral-wallpapered hallway to the kitchen, where I was delighted to see no tea ready to be served—no cake, pudding, or home-baked cookies I simply must try. Vera, at least, didn't take to sweetening up her judges with treats.

And speaking of treats, Milton was sleeping in the corner. I had to go over to him and stroke his fur before he raised his head and sniffed me. Then his tail began to thump the flag-stone floor.

"Here you go, boy," I said, offering him a liver snack.

He made short work of the three treats and then sniffed the floor hopefully for crumbs.

I looked around me properly. I was wowed by a double set of French doors which opened to the garden.

"My little pride and joy," Vera said as we stepped into the late-afternoon sunshine.

I followed her, and I could see why.

Her back garden was a real English country garden, a jumble of color. Small, yes, but perfect. And with the most delightful array of roses. The borders, in particular, were wonderful examples of a relaxed cottage style. As I took it all in, I noted the Félicité-Perpétue—small, closely packed pompon flowers of creamy white with pink flushes which bloomed in slightly hanging clusters. I couldn't resist sniffing the delicate fragrance. The garden wall was covered in a burst of Malvern Hill roses bearing fully double, soft yellow blooms. Theirs was a medium musky fragrance.

There were also several of the modern strain of roses, grown to be more disease-resistant.

"This is the Jubilee Celebration rose," Vera said, pointing to a pink bush bursting with blooms and popular with the bees. "In honor of our late Queen."

While I was admiring the roses, Neil walked into the garden, looking relaxed in a pair of jeans and a white linen shirt. He must have worked from home today. "Ah, Peony," he said on seeing me.

"Neil's such a help in the garden," Vera said in a proud tone. "I couldn't do it without him."

Milton wandered out of the house, sniffed the garden air, and sneezed.

Neil said, "I know my grandmother's garden isn't as large or fancy as some, but I personally find it more authentic." Though he didn't mention whose garden he had in mind as a comparison, I suspected it was Colleen O'Brien's.

"Vera's roses are amazing," I said, trying to be diplomatic.

"There are so many variations of the English rose that once I started with one, I couldn't help myself. I just kept going. Each rose offers its own unique beauty, don't you think?" She dreamily surveyed her garden. With a whimsical expression, she added, "I do so like to nurture a garden. To think about how it will be when I'm gone. How the next generation of custodians will tend to the blooms." We both glanced at Neil.

No doubt this would one day be his to maintain.

I hoped that would be a long time in the future, and I suspected Neil did, too.

He said, "You've created something timeless." Surely this was really the point of the competition? Not winning, but creating something beautiful for everyone—from neighbors to butterflies and bees—to enjoy and tend?

I excused myself to take a better look, snapping photos and adding notes to my clipboard. Walking around, I was immediately soothed by Vera's garden. Erica and Greg's zen garden might have been designed with meditative qualities in mind, but personally, I found this one far more soothing. Maybe not having an active feud with the neighbors helped. And now Vera's grandson and his family were her neighbors. How perfect. I was thrilled for Vera.

As I strolled, Milton found his way to me and nudged my

knee with his head. I think that dog associated me with treats. I bent to stroke his soft head. "No more treats today, my friend."

Milton seemed to understand and dropped down in the sunny grass, resting his head between his paws.

Vera and Neil had taken a seat on the patio and appeared to be lost in their own conversation rather than watching me like a hawk as the others had done. It was a refreshing change. As I approached unnoticed, I realized they were talking about the dig next door. Maybe I could get the scoop on the latest.

"All I'm saying is that digger starts earlier than the baby," Neil was saying, shaking his head.

Vera shrugged. "Honestly, I sleep through it."

"I don't know how. It's like someone drilling a hole in my temples."

Vera laughed. "Surely you're used to worse sounds after living in central London so long?"

I smiled and took a seat. With all the excitement of discovering archaeological treasures, I'd not considered how annoying it must be to live next to the dig.

"And the skeleton they found?" Neil shivered. "You know they've taken to calling him Caesar?"

"I found it quite amusing, myself," Vera said. "Although the thought of living next to an ancient burial for so long *is* unsettling." She turned to me with a bright smile. "You must be thirsty, Peony." It was more of a statement than a question. "After a long day judging *and* working," she added. Vera gave me a mischievous look. "And since the sun is going down, I think it would be rude not to have a little sherry, don't you?"

I dredged up a grateful look. Sherry was not my drink, but

she seemed so pleased to have me here that I didn't like to disappoint her. Vera disappeared into the cottage and emerged with a plate of fruitcake and two small glasses of sherry.

Fruitcake.

And sweet sherry.

I bit into a slab of cake and recalled a meme a friend had posted at Christmas about the fourth wise man who was never heard from again. He brought fruitcake.

However, whatever my personal feelings about fruitcake, I was a huge fan of Vera's garden. I loved the heirloom roses, the hum of bees, the casual way the flowers all grew together. Personally, I loved this garden the best of the four I'd visited today.

Not least because there was no anger, bitterness, or animosity hanging over the space.

When I left, Neil walked me out. "I know it's not my business," he said as we reached my car, "but it would be so nice to see someone win this year who cares more about the garden itself than showing off for their neighbors."

While I completely understood his position, I also felt it was inappropriate for him to try to influence me. And I'd discovered the downside of judging a local contest. Whoever won would think I was wonderful.

But depending on who came out not a winner, I suspected I'd make at least one enemy.

BACK HOME, I breathed a sigh of relief that the day was over. No more visits, no more chats, no more snacks. With any luck, Char and Hilary would be out, my mom would be at her own place for once, and Blue and I could curl up together and read the evening away.

Of course, best-laid plans and all that.

I'd only been in the house a few minutes when I heard the roar of an engine coming from Char's garage. Char was home, and what's more, she was either tinkering with Frodo or another car from her growing list of clients.

I went outside to check on Char and stopped to enjoy my own garden. Okay, it was far from perfect, but it was beautiful in its own way. I moved toward my namesake peonies, which Owen had moved to get them to grow better and bloom. Now that they got the morning light, they were much happier. For the most part, they'd finished blooming now, but there was one bush with a late bloom that I'd been enjoying. It was a deep pink with a delicate fragrance. I turned my gaze that way and let out a gasp of shock.

Standing by the bloom, as though she were enjoying its fragrance, was Yasmin, the garden gnome. I shook my head. How could that be? Without Char to pick her up and bring her to the farmhouse, I'd left the gnome sitting by the cash register at Bewitching Blooms.

I strode closer, shading my eyes against the sinking sun. That was definitely Yasmin by my peony bush. How had she got over there?

I crouched down and stared into her pretty blue eyes. There was something knowing about her expression, which I hadn't noticed before. It was like we shared a secret.

I got a hold of myself. Char must have returned to my shop and decided to bring Yasmin back here. It seemed like my housemate was letting me know that she'd like us to purchase the gnome for the farmhouse. It wasn't a terrible idea. Yasmin did look as though she belonged.

I turned to go find Char and tell her Yasmin could stay when I heard the sound of a throat clearing. I spun around. No one was there.

"Char?" I called out.

"You must water the ground more thoroughly. The soil's dry beneath the surface." The voice sounded like it belonged to a young woman. Sweet and well-spoken.

I looked around for Char again. Was she playing tricks on me? Some kind of new magic she'd stumbled upon without my knowledge?

But no.

There was no one there but the gnome.

Surely not.

I crouched down again, certain now it was *my* mind playing tricks on me. I peered at Yasmin's face, narrowing my gaze. The blue eyes stared back at me.

No. Couldn't be.

I was about to head back to the house when the voice spoke again. "Evening is best, so the sun doesn't dry out the ground before the water can seep down. But not too late, mind you. And if you forget, early morning is good, too, before the sun is up."

What the—? I stared at the gnome again, utterly bemused.

"Peony?" The voice came from behind me, and I spun around.

This time it *was* Char. I breathed a sigh of relief. As she came closer, I saw that her cheek and hair were smeared with engine oil.

"What are you doing?" she asked. "Because from here, it looks like you were talking to a garden gnome."

I lowered my voice. "This might sound crazy, but I swear I heard her speak." I paused for a second. "She was giving me gardening advice."

We both turned to observe the gnome, who looked inanimate now, her eyes blankly staring, her lips painted shut. To my surprise, Char didn't let out an enormous cackle. She blinked twice and then blew out a breath.

"Um," she started, and then stopped. "I don't think you're crazy."

I looked from Char to the gnome and back again, then my witch intuition kicked in. "Did she talk to you, too?"

She tucked a strand of oily hair behind her ear. "I think I might have brought her to life yesterday. Accidentally, of course."

"You brought Yasmin to life?"

"I think so," Char said. She went on to explain that she had been practicing her spell to spark Frodo's engine without having to turn the key in the ignition when things got a little out of hand. "I think I lost control of the direction of my spell. Next thing I knew, I saw the gnome tip its watering can and water a dry-looking flower."

"She was watering the garden?" I had to repeat the words to make certain I'd heard correctly.

"Yep. The flower immediately perked up. Turns out she knows a thing or two about gardens."

I stared at Char. And then I remembered: she'd had a sudden reaction to something happening in the garden this morning. I'd figured she was crushing on Owen in the garden, but really she'd seen a gnome water a flower by itself.

"Why didn't you tell me?" I asked. Although I'd warned Char to be careful with her burgeoning magic, I wasn't about to get mad when things didn't go to plan. Mistakes happened. We just had to be honest about them. I said as much to Char, and she blushed.

"I was worried about getting in trouble. Thought maybe I could fix it myself."

"Two witches are always better than one," I said. "You should already know that."

I turned back to Yasmin. "So you made your own way home? Really? That's a lot of walking for a little lady."

Yasmin's eyes blinked to life. "I did not wish to be alone."

Char gasped.

"We are social creatures," Yasmin continued in her sweet, pure voice.

Both Char and I bent down and studied the gnome. "Do you need a friend?" I asked. I wondered if I could find a suitable match for her in the catalog, kind of like online dating for gnomes.

"I have friends, thank you. Though few are as empathetic as you are. Some people put us in sunny spots even when we prefer shade, and far from each other so we can't talk easily. It's very unkind when we do so much to help your gardens grow."

"Wait," Char said, "you mean other gnomes can talk, too?"

"Of course," Yasmin said sweetly. "We all have spirits. Not everything is about your magic."

Char's expression was a study in astonishment. She glanced at me. "So it wasn't my fault. I didn't bring her to life."

"You most certainly did not," Yasmin said with dignity. "You didn't create me, you heard me. There's a difference."

"Can I get you anything?" Char asked. Now that she was growing used to the idea that Yasmin was more than an inanimate object, she seemed fascinated.

"Why, thank you for asking. I do love butterflies. They are so pretty and sometimes they land on me, which we consider good luck. Sadly, there aren't as many as there used to be, and we must do what we can to feed and encourage them. You've got some wild marjoram growing in the herb garden, and that's very good. But I'd like to see some verbena, lovely purple Hebe, which also attracts bees, of course. Such lovely nectar. And—"

"Wait," Char cried, digging out her phone. "I have to make a note or I'll forget."

"Verbena," she repeated, typing into her phone, "and Hebe. Okay, what else?"

"Valerian." Yasmin looked at me. "Which you might know as moon-root or cat's paw. I was surprised not to see it in your witch's garden."

I could have told her I'd had a patch, but it died, but decided to hold my tongue. I didn't want this tiny garden expert to think she and her watering can could find more fertile ground in which to live. I liked her and wanted her to stay. I resolved to get some valerian from another witch (so much more powerful than anything I could buy from a nursery) and put more effort into growing plants that would attract as many butterflies as I could to my garden.

I was about to tell Yasmin that her friends were always welcome, but I had a feeling I'd be wasting my breath. No doubt they met often when most of us were asleep.

CHAPTER 12

Sunday passed pleasantly, but too quickly. I visited Amanda and came away not only with a nice potful of valerian but also a recipe for a tonic to aid sleep.

"Keep the valerian in the pot, though, Peony," Amanda warned. "Or it will take over your garden."

I didn't tell her I'd somehow managed to accidentally eradicate my first valerian. It seemed humiliating to admit I'd managed to kill an invasive plant. Amanda also sent me home with some mugwort. I went into my garden to add them and found Yasmin nestled among the lavender. Blue was curled on the new stone pavers sleeping in the sun.

Remembering Amanda's advice, I set the pot of valerian down in the shade of a gangly Rosemary bush, but Yasmin tutted. "It wants more sun." Following her direction, I moved it to a sunny spot in front of the lavender. "Valerian will do well in poorer soil, though perhaps it's as well in the pot. Don't worry. I shall keep an eye on it."

When Yasmin saw the mugwort, she said, "Ah, lovely.

Artemis Herb. Yes, that will grow nicely beside the bay tree. I shall keep an eye on it, too."

It was nice having a resident garden expert, even if she was smaller than most of the herb bushes she sat amongst. She seemed to love that spot, with the buzz of contented bees, and to my delight, a butterfly circled and then lighted on her bonnet.

The garden competition committee spent Sunday evening trimming the entries and weeding out the ones who wouldn't make the semi-finals. (A garden competition does lend itself to puns). Of the eighteen entries, we hoped to prune the number to six finalists. That was one for each of us and two extras. I struggled to get my four down to two and in the end decided that Greg and Erica Lawley would be disappointed. It wasn't that I hadn't loved their zen garden. I did, but when I added up my score sheets, Vera came out on top, which made me happy. Colleen O'Brien was only a point or two lower, and the Lawleys a couple of points lower still. Elizabeth Sanderson's garden had been pleasant, but not outstanding.

Justine had only visited one garden that she scored high enough for the finals but—like me—Arthur and Bernard both had two. To get to six finalists, I suggested that maybe Colleen O'Brien should be left out this year, but the two men were aghast.

"No, indeed," said Arthur. "Why, Colleen's garden is a treasure. It's bad enough she's got to do it alone. Now that her husband's off in Ireland looking after his mother, we can't take her out of the finals."

I wanted to remind them that Elizabeth tended her garden on her own—and that I wasn't sure someone like

Colleen, who was suspected of tree sabotage, should be allowed to be a finalist, but I kept my mouth shut.

Bernard mentioned that he'd noticed a patch of noxious weed growing in one corner of an otherwise spectacular garden, and that was enough to cut his list down to one, now. He was only putting forward the garden of a family called the Tewksburys.

We'd all visit the remaining six gardens as a group to make the final decisions.

"Good," Arthur said. "Now that we've got our list of finalists, we'll have the traditional press conference tomorrow. I'm personally acquainted with the editor of *The Willow Waters Weekly*." Honestly, he made the announcement as though he personally knew the editor of *The New York Times*. "She will print our list," Arthur continued, "after she and her photographer visit each garden to take pictures and interview the finalists."

I often glanced through the local paper, which was delivered to the farmhouse every week. I imagined all the locals did.

"Peony," Arthur said, "wouldn't it be nice to have the press conference in your shop, with all those beautiful flowers as a backdrop?"

"What a good idea," Bernard said.

If I didn't know them both, I'd have suspected they'd rehearsed this.

"We're holding a press conference at Bewitching Blooms tomorrow," I repeated, to make sure I was hearing this right.

"Yes, what excellent publicity for your shop," Arthur said, beaming at me.

And because he was right, I agreed.

BEFORE I KNEW IT, I was back at Bewitching Blooms, busy with Monday orders.

And I'd discovered I'd be holding a press conference to let the local newspaper know which gardens had made the finals.

So this Monday was even busier than usual. On top of my weekly orders and account management, I wanted to get the shop floor gleaming and looking beautiful. Arthur had sent a press release to the BBC and a few larger papers, hoping they'd send someone, but even if it was only our local paper who attended, I was determined to show off Bewitching Blooms at its best.

Normally, I got up super early and went to the wholesaler to buy stock on Monday mornings, but Imogen agreed to go in my stead. I say agreed, but in fact she was eager. I was slightly nervous. In all the time we'd worked together, I had always been the one to visit the wholesaler, browse through the nurseries, and pick the most delectable stems for my discerning customers. It was one of the top pleasures of running the shop. But this morning, it was Imogen's job.

Once I'd wrapped my head around relinquishing control, I was glad that Imogen was progressing in the business. I was lucky to have her, and if I wanted to keep her, I was going to have to let her blossom. (Again with the puns.)

Norman was with Char today, and I'd warned him not to come into Bewitching Blooms. I didn't think a smart-mouthed parrot was a great addition to a press conference. However, Yasmin was back beside my till. She liked being outside in my garden, but she was lonely there. Besides, when she perched beside the till, I got more orders for the locally-handcrafted gnomes, so it was a win-win. She had me for company, and I got more orders.

I was worried about bringing her into my shop in case her mouth accidentally ran away with her, but she assured me she would be seen and not heard.

Imogen arrived early with the flower order, and I was immediately reassured. She'd done a great job and beamed when I told her so. We set about filling buckets, putting some slightly-past-their-prime blooms in the free bucket outside, and then she got to work on the flower orders that had come in on Sunday.

When my first customer rolled in at 10 a.m., I felt like I'd already done a day's work. I vaguely recognized the woman as one I'd seen before. I thought she lived locally but didn't come in too often. I put on my brightest smile and helped her choose pink roses, mixed with long stems of iris, and a few fern fronds. The commercially-grown roses didn't have the glorious scent of Vera's roses, and I wished I could stock those.

The woman bent to admire Yasmin. Then she read the brochure sitting beside the gnome. "My, she's a pricey little thing, isn't she?"

"The gnomes are handmade locally. Each has a unique personality." More than this woman could possibly imagine.

"She's got such an expressive face. Lovely." Then she straightened.

"Are these for a special occasion?" I asked as I wrapped her flowers in paper.

"My mother," she said. "My father died last week, and she's having a rough time. They doted on each other."

I had a lot of sympathy for the widow, having suffered that grief myself. As I turned to the tape dispenser to finish the wrapping, I whispered:

> *"Let these blooms heal and lift the heart*
> *And bring peace to this loving wife, now torn apart.*
> *As lonely as a mourning dove,*
> *Let her be comforted by a daughter's love.*
> *So I will, so mote it be."*

On impulse, I took a single pink rose and a bit of fern and handed it to the daughter. "You're grieving, too," I reminded her. "So I want you to have something as well."

"Oh, that's so nice of you," she said, and her eyes welled with tears. "Thank you. Even though he was old and it was his time, I've still lost my daddy."

"I know."

She touched Yasmin's bonnet, almost for good luck, and said, "Perhaps I'll come back and get one of these."

"There's a catalog. You can choose the one you want."

She nodded and left. I let the moment of sadness wash through me as I thought of Jeremy. Then, I got back to work.

It wasn't long before my shop's bell announced that I had another visitor.

Wiping my hands on my apron, I fixed a welcoming smile on my face and turned toward the door.

Now you'll have to take my word for it, but it took all my willpower to keep that smile intact when Colleen O'Brien walked in.

"Morning, Colleen," I said as brightly as I could muster. "What a surprise."

Colleen did not return my pleasant smile. As she swept in, she brought a wave of negative energy with her. I'd have to smudge my shop before the press conference for sure, or everyone in the media would pick up the negative vibes. Her face was fixed in a scowl, her skin pale gray—as if she hadn't slept a wink. I swallowed, unsure how to proceed. The obvious choice would be to ask if she was okay, but something told me I did not want the answer to that question.

I took up a position behind the counter. I felt safer there, with a little distance between us—and Yasmin by my side, silly as that might seem. I quickly envisaged a beautiful rose growing in front of me. Gorgeous, but also strong and thorny. It was for psychic protection.

Colleen strode through my shop toward me. A woman on a mission. A mission to complain. As soon as she got close to me, she let rip. "It's those awful neighbors of mine, Peony," she said, as if we were old friends. "They've been torturing me."

"Torturing?" I murmured. With what? A meditation gong?

She let out a gigantic huff. "They've been sneaking into my garden at night and moving my precious gnomes around. You saw it on Saturday. My flute player was in the wrong spot. Naturally, I believed I must have made the mistake, but I didn't. This morning, they'd all switched positions. It looks completely wrong. All wrong."

I didn't dare so much as glance at Yasmin. I doubted very much that Colleen's neighbors had anything to do with gnomes who moved as if by magic.

I didn't know what to say, so I remained silent, not wanting to encourage her. I felt my psychic protection was struggling to keep out her bad energy.

"Those two city heathens are sabotaging my chances at winning the best-garden award this year. I'm convinced of it. If my husband was here, they wouldn't dare, but I'm all alone and vulnerable." Her speech was gathering momentum now, swelling and pitching like an angry ocean. Her pale skin had flushed red.

I had no clue what to say. I would have to choose my words carefully so that I didn't become her next target. "Why would they do that?" I asked gingerly. "Your gnome arrangement is delightful, but it's by no means the most important aspect of your garden. What would they stand to gain?" Little did Colleen know that she almost hadn't made the finals.

Colleen scowled again and her voice turned firm. "I thought you should know that they are meddling. In fact, I'm making an official complaint. I want Greg and Erica Lawley disqualified from the competition."

This put me in a very awkward position. I already knew the Lawleys hadn't made the finals, but I couldn't tell Colleen that. She would read the list of finalists along with everyone else in *The Willow Waters Weekly*.

I tried to reason with her. "First of all, you need proof of your accusation." Which I knew was most likely untrue. If anyone was playing a prank on Colleen O'Brien, I suspected it was the gnomes themselves. "Have you got CCTV footage or—?"

But Colleen wasn't open to reason. She cut me off before I even finished my question. "I'm going to get back at those two if it's the last thing I do."

"Now, Colleen, I understand emotions are running high, but there's no need for threats. Whatever's been going on with the gnomes," I said while still trying not to so much as glance at Yasmin, "it won't affect the judging."

Colleen was not one for listening. She began her tirade all over again, and I was helpless to block the torrent. I glanced at the brilliant sunshine outside the window, wondering where my hopeful morning had disappeared to, when I saw Justine walking down the street. I made a small motion to wave the vicar inside.

Colleen O'Brien was so deep into her rant she didn't notice my gesture. I was nodding and trying not to use my magic to push her out the door, when she leaned closer to me, her face mottled with fury, "I'm a peaceful woman, but If they don't stop their campaign to destroy me, I'll destroy them."

THE WORDS 'I'LL DESTROY THEM' seemed to hang in the air. Fortunately, Justine had seen my gesture and came into my shop. Colleen had the good sense to pause her rant when the door chimed and immediately perked up when she saw another judge. I wanted Justine to diffuse the tension, not provide another excuse for Colleen to spew more fury.

"Vicar," Colleen said, extending a hand in greeting. I couldn't help noticing that I didn't receive her polite hand-shake greeting. "I'm so glad to catch you. I've been explaining to Peony that I'm having a spot of bother with the competition."

Justine shot me a look like *why-did-you-drag-me-into-this-Peony*, but then her kind features relaxed into their usual caring smile. She managed to keep that smile while Colleen eagerly began recounting her woes for a second time.

Justine placed a hand on Colleen's arm and invited her to the rectory for a cup of tea. Happily, Colleen appeared flattered by the invitation, and the two of them left.

I watched as they disappeared down the high street, grateful to Justine for her kindness. I could see more customers coming toward me on the high street. So, instead of taking the time to smudge my shop, I opened the door and pictured white, cleansing light filling the space and pushing out the dark energy. There was a sound like a whoosh, and when I felt the bad atmosphere was cleansed, I retraced my steps to the counter, pleased to feel a lightness in the air.

I put my face close to Yasmin's. I could swear I saw her eyes twinkling.

"Do you know anything about gnomes playing tricks on Colleen O'Brien?" I asked.

"Normally, gnomes return to where they've been placed," Yasmin admitted. "But if they're not in a happy home, they might not be so worried about their human's feelings."

I bet that was exactly why Colleen's gnomes were moving around at night—they were dissatisfied with their environment and were trying to make themselves more comfortable. But it wasn't like I could tell Colleen that her gnomes—and not her neighbors—were playing tricks on her.

Yasmin said, "That was an angry woman. And such deep anger isn't good for anyone."

The gnome's words were the most sensible thing I'd heard all morning.

But Colleen O'Brien's threat against her neighbors was definitely the most disturbing.

WHEN THE TIME grew near for the press conference, Imogen announced that she was taking her lunch break. I wouldn't have minded if she stayed, but it would be less crowded without her. The shop looked and smelled wonderful, my precious blooms plentiful and impressively arranged, if I do say so myself.

I found time to brush my hair and swipe some lipstick on, then I put a clean apron over my jeans and cotton shirt.

"You look very nice," Yasmin said from beside the till.

I'd half forgotten she was there. It was kind of like having Norman around, except Yasmin was much nicer. And more polite.

"Why, thank you," I said.

"I wish I could change dresses," she said whimsically. "I do get tired of this one."

"Well, I think your dress is very pretty," I said, and then covered my comment with a loud cough—the door had chimed, and I didn't want a reporter catching me talking to a gnome.

In walked a woman and a man from our local paper. I'd seen them both at events around the village but never properly met them.

"Hi," said the solid woman, who was on the short side, had freckles, and appeared to be in her fifties. "I'm Darcie Crane, the editor of *The Willow Waters Weekly*. I'm also its only reporter." Her hazel eyes blinked behind clear square frames as she pulled a notebook from her bag. "We manage on a skeleton staff."

"And I'm Felix, our paper's only photographer," the man

said. He was his coworker's opposite. Tall and very thin, he had a sweet look about him, like a puppy, with large trusting eyes and sloping shoulders, as if he were trying to disguise his height. Or maybe it was the heavy-looking camera hanging on a strap around his neck that weighed him down.

Darcie scanned my shop. "It must be nice to work with flowers," she said, as she bent to inspect the red roses. "If I worked here every day, instead of my tiny cubicle, I'm sure I'd be at least eighty percent happier." She sighed. "Or if I had someone in my life sending me your flowers, I'd be happier."

"Lots of people buy flowers for themselves," I reminded her. "A little self-love goes a long way."

She nodded. "Thanks for announcing the finalists on a Monday. It means we'll catch Thursday's edition of the paper. And this is big news in Willow Waters."

I must have looked surprised, for she said, "People don't read our paper for hard news. They get that on the telly and in the dailies. Our job is to report on the things that matter right here. What the local council is up to, celebrity sightings, Women's Institute events, that kind of thing."

"I read it every week," I told her. For all those reasons she'd just said. If you wanted to find out what was happening in the village, *The Willow Waters Weekly* would tell you.

Justine arrived with Arthur and Bernard. They greeted Darcie and Felix, then Arthur glanced around as though the BBC cameras might be hiding behind the sunflowers. We'd agreed that Arthur would announce the finalists, though really, in the absence of any other media, he was only giving the list of finalists to Darcie.

I put a sign on the door saying the shop would be closed for thirty minutes.

We judges had all made an effort. Arthur and Bernard sported freshly ironed shirts and neat hair, while Justine wore a skirt and jacket. Like me, she'd recently brushed her hair and added some lipstick.

Darcie first got all of our names with the correct spelling. I recalled the old saying, 'I don't care what you say about me, but spell my name right.'

Then Darcie asked, "How difficult was the competition this year?"

Arthur immediately launched into praise of the wonderful gardens in Willow Waters and how proud we should be of all the green thumbs. "I wish everyone who entered could have won."

Since Justine and I were new, Darcie asked us how it had felt to be a judge. If I'd told the truth, I'd have said I wished I'd never said yes to be one. Instead, I talked about how inspiring it was to see all the different ways local residents turned a plot of earth into their own amazing vision.

Darcie nodded, attentive and professional. When she'd finished her questions, she called over Felix, who was busy taking close-ups of some particularly pretty delphiniums.

He looked sheepish. "I'm a bit of a nature lover, myself," he confessed. "Trees are my thing. I have a walking group that goes all around the Cotswolds, but I'm always getting left behind, taking photos."

He asked us to stand in front of my wall of flowers.

Then he snapped and snapped, giving us directions as he changed positions. We were all to look at the sheet of finalists as though discussing who should win. Justine tilted her head to the right; Arthur stood up straighter; I was instructed to stop frowning, which only furrowed my brow more. Then he got us to move around the shop, so he had different backgrounds. I tried to keep a smile fixed on my face, but by now my cheeks were aching.

Darcie asked each of us to give our thoughts about what the competition's purpose was.

"It's great for village morale," Arthur said. "Everyone working together to beautify our gorgeous part of the world."

Justine said, "Spending time in a beautiful garden is good for the soul."

I knew my answer to this one. "Flowers bring joy to people's lives."

Bernard looked stumped and chuckled. "Why, you've said it all." He asked for a few moments to think, then suddenly burst out, "But for me, this is about a fun and friendly competition between neighbors."

Fun and friendly? He obviously hadn't spent time with Colleen O'Brien.

"I can take a few photos of just you in your store if you'd like," Felix said to me. "You can use them for advertising or marketing."

I was delighted. Getting some decent photos I could use in promotions would be fantastic and I told him so. The other judges took their leave, and Darcie followed them out. Felix spent a few minutes taking pictures of me in front of my flower displays, pretending to arrange a quick bouquet and, finally, outside in front of the open door. I'd become so used to having my photo taken by this time that I was pretty relaxed.

When he was finished, I thanked him profusely. "I hate having my picture taken, but you made it easy."

"I'm surprised. You're very photogenic. Want to have a look?" he asked.

I nodded, although part of me dreaded the results. I stood beside him as he flicked back through his pictures. There were definitely one or two of me that I could use. Absently, he flicked back through the group shots, and I fought the urge to burst out laughing. No matter the angle, Yasmin appeared in the background of every photograph.

The gnome was beside the till, then she was just visible behind the roses, and there she was in the shadow of the doorway. I really hoped no one else would notice. Otherwise I'd have to pretend I'd been moving her around.

"You should think about joining our walking group," Felix said shyly. "I think you'd enjoy it. We call ourselves the Walkie-Talkies. It's all pretty informal." He gave me his work card and said to email him if I'd like to join one weekend.

I thanked him. What a nice idea.

He left and a minute later Imogen returned, bringing me a much-needed coffee and sandwich. She must have kept an eye out for everyone to leave. "How was it?" she asked.

"Fine. But I'm glad the contest will be over soon." I sipped the coffee, then told her, "Colleen O'Brien came in earlier."

Imogen screwed up her face. "What did she want?"

"She thinks her garden's being sabotaged by her neighbors."

"Argh. Not again. That woman has a seriously heavy chip on her shoulder."

I agreed. Despite the pleasant morning outside, I couldn't shake the darkness Colleen had brought with her into my shop. "She actually threatened her neighbors."

"With what?" Imogen asked.

I shrugged. "Her threats were vague and disturbing."

"Do you think she's serious?"

"That depends on whether she killed the Lawleys' tree or not."

I unwrapped my sandwich and bit into it. It was a healthy veggie sandwich on whole wheat bread, but Roberto's sandwiches were never ordinary. This one had some kind of Italian aioli, and the veggies had been roasted. It was fantastic. Not even thoughts of Colleen O'Brien could dampen my appetite.

Imogen put her apron back on and settled down to work. "It's a long way from killing a tree to hurting a human being," she said.

"I suppose you're right. I'll put her behavior down to stress."

And I could only hope that's all it was.

I forgot all about Colleen O'Brien when Alex came into Bewitching Blooms.

He greeted both of us and said, "It always smells especially good in here on Mondays. The flowers are so fresh."

"Did you just come in here to...stop and smell the roses?" I teased.

"As a matter of fact, I'm here on business." Seeing my obvious surprise, he said, "George and Annabel are celebrating their wedding anniversary. I thought I'd send them flowers."

"What a lovely thought," Imogen said.

"I don't know what kind of flowers, though. Can I leave it to you, Imogen?"

"Of course," she said, glancing from him to me to him

again, with a hopeful look. "Do you want someone to deliver them?"

Imogen was playing Cupid.

Alex paused before saying, "Perhaps, Peony, you could bring them after work tomorrow and then I could take you for dinner."

Imogen looked pretty pleased with herself, and I nodded in agreement. I thought this was an excellent plan—and I appreciated Imogen's nudge to get Alex to take the next step. A date with him was exactly what I needed to keep Colleen O'Brien and her nastiness out of my mind.

CHAPTER 13

Imogen made a gorgeous bouquet for Alex's butler, George, and his wife, and I imbued the blooms with added joy for the special occasion.

I parked at Alex's, noting the difference in the grounds. He must have hired a team of gardeners to get so much done so quickly. I was admiring the smooth lawn and freshly-trimmed hedges when Alex came out the front door.

He gave me a quick kiss and then took the flowers. "George and Annabel are going out tonight too, so I'll give them the flowers before they leave." He seemed so happy, I was reminded that George was more family than servant.

He quickly returned, and rather than taking my Range Rover, we drove to the restaurant in his much sleeker and more expensive Jaguar.

"I made a reservation at a pub. I hope that's all right."

"Of course." I didn't expect a fancy meal every time we went out.

However, when we pulled up to The Unicorn, it was obvious that this was no ordinary pub. Old, quaint, and picturesque it might be, but on walking in, there was a feeling of quiet wealth coming from the patrons, the décor, and even the servers. I tended to forget that Alex was Lord Fitzlupin, but at times like this, I was reminded that he was landed gentry. The maître d' said how good it was to see his lordship again and led us to what must have been the best table in the house.

"Wow," I said. "This isn't just any pub. What's the occasion?"

"Spending time together, as I'll soon be out of action for a day or two."

I knew what he meant. He couldn't trust himself to be in public for the two days around the full moon. Safely ensconced in his castle, he would ask his butler and friend George to keep him under lock and key in the old dungeon until the moon began to wane and Alex was safely human again. Or so he'd told me.

I'd been firmly banned from coming near him during those times. Alex wanted me to know his human side. And since I was more of a cat person, I didn't put up an argument. It was one of those bridges we'd cross when the time came.

The Unicorn's menu wasn't large, but everything was organic and local. They cooked what was in season, and the chef was up-and-coming famous.

I settled on a salad made from greens picked that day, followed by spaghetti with local mushrooms in some kind of fancy sauce.

Alex ordered wine and then admitted that his company stocked all the vintages here.

"Which shows they have good taste," I said.

He started with scallops flown in that day from Cornwall, followed by rare steak.

We chatted about our days. I caught him up on the garden committee, though I couldn't tell him who the finalists were. He'd find out with everyone else when *The Willow Waters Weekly* came out.

I found myself telling him about seeing Gillian with Greg Lawley. "It's not that they were doing anything shocking, but why were the two of them really in her garden? Gillian said he was teaching her to meditate, but they were holding hands."

"She does like to bring trouble on herself, doesn't she?"

"You know I'm not one for prying," I said to Alex, twirling a slick forkful of spaghetti around my fork before bringing it to my mouth. "But I feel like someone should warn her to stay away from Greg Lawley. He already has trouble at home."

Alex raised a brow. By now, I knew that look.

I laughed. "Come on, it's not prying. It's genuine concern for human beings."

"That, I don't doubt. But when it comes to Gillian, it's easy to jump to conclusions. Maybe she truly is learning to meditate."

"It's just that Gillian doesn't strike me as the type to get into meditation," I said, shaking my head at Alex's offer of some escalope. "She likes luxury cars, lavish houses, expensive fabrics. She's as material as you get."

"Are you suggesting rich people can't meditate?" He looked amused at the idea.

"No. It's not that. But Greg Lawley was into minimalism and Zen, or he said he was. And Gillian's never seemed to have much interest in her inner life. Does that make sense?"

"You think she and Greg Lawley are having an affair?"

"I don't know."

Gillian didn't exactly help herself. She was always being linked to men: her tennis coach, an old flame suddenly back in town, a random boyfriend with a murderous jealous side. The woman didn't learn. As I've said before, I had a soft spot for Gillian. I knew what it was like to be an outsider. I knew what it was like to be a widow. But one thing I couldn't relate to was the need for attention from the opposite sex.

Since I'd seen her and Greg in Lemmington House's garden, I'd been worried. I'd sensed an intensity between them I couldn't quite put my finger on. It didn't feel like the electric charge of lovers—the frisson I felt when I looked at Alex right now. But I didn't think it was purely a meditation session, either.

Alex nodded and sipped wine. I followed suit. It really was a beautiful wine.

"Perhaps she's trying to change," Alex said. "Who expected Gillian to want to join the WI, for instance? Yet there she is, every meeting. Even when no one is talking to her."

"How do *you* know what goes on at the WI?" I asked.

Alex's eyes sparkled. "Oh, I hear things," he said cryptically.

I could tell he wasn't going to reveal his sources. However, even though he was both the richest man in town and the highest born, I'd seen Alex chatting to villagers he met on the high street or in the coffee shop or pub. No doubt he was as caught up on village gossip as anyone.

And he was right. Gillian had indeed immersed herself in the world of the Women's Institute, attending cake sales and crochet circles and even trying her hand at ikebana one month, or so I'd been told—people did like to talk about Gillian. She was trying to fit in here in Willow Waters in her beautiful country estate, but she always gave the impression that she really belonged on yachts and private islands where secretive billionaires lurked.

"She wanted to be accepted by the community," I said. "I'm not sure closing your eyes and meditating will help in Willow Waters."

Alex looked thoughtful. He looked handsome, too, in case you were wondering.

Alex gestured at my wine glass and asked what I thought of the Bordeaux. I thought it was pretty good. He never pushed his knowledge on me, but when I asked about the wine we were drinking, he was generous with his knowledge. I was getting able to tell the difference between a merlot and a Malbec, for instance, which tickled me. I think Alex was quite proud, too. I'd never have his nose, for obvious reasons, nor did I particularly want to, but it was nice to learn a bit about wine.

"I'm not so sure Gillian's all that concerned with the meditation part of meditating, anyway," Alex said.

I shot him a quizzical look.

"I bumped into Owen Jones at Roberto's earlier," he said. "He was on his way to the gardening center to buy materials for Lemmington House. Gillian has decided to build a meditation garden. I was taken aback. As you said, Gillian and Zen aren't two things I'd put together. But on reflection, maybe she's more into the aesthetics of the garden than the actual meditating. She does seem to like a home improvement project. Owen is always running around trying to satisfy her next whim. I can absolutely believe this is just a new passion project."

"That makes sense," I said, feeling somewhat relieved. "Maybe Greg is just helping her with her garden." I hoped this was the case, but I didn't quite believe my own optimism.

"How did Gillian's lunch go?" I asked, suspecting Owen would have told Alex. Even though Gillian would probably pretend my flowers were from her garden, I liked knowing my bouquet had been the centerpiece.

"What lunch?"

"Gillian was giving a lunch on Sunday," I told him. Maybe he didn't know everything that went on, after all.

"I don't think so. Owen said Gillian was away for a few days. She left Sunday morning. And left him with instructions to get started on her meditation garden while she was gone."

"That's strange," I said. She'd definitely been planning a luncheon when she ordered a bouquet on Saturday. "She must have been called away."

But Alex didn't know anything more.

Even though we were miles from home, I lowered my voice. "I know this will stay between us, but when I left Colleen and went next door to Erica and Greg's, their garden was tranquil, but their marriage was not. They were snappy and short with each other. Let's just say it was awkward."

Alex sat back in his chair with a wry smile. "Ah, yes, the garden competition. I was wondering when you would bring that up. It's not as simple as you'd hoped, is it?"

I scrunched my nose. I hated to admit it, but the competition *was* more than I'd bargained for. But maybe not for the reasons Alex thought. I shook my head. "Believe me when I say I can handle a lot of stuff, which might surprise you." I paused for dramatic effect. "What I'm finding difficult is learning about what goes on behind closed doors. I mean, most of us keep doors closed for a reason. There are things about my fellow villagers that I don't want to know."

"Has it been bad?"

"Yes and no." I explained how uncomfortable it was to bear witness to domestic nastiness. Nothing major, no huge fights or bouts of temper. No, it was the simmering quality of palpable tensions bubbling away beneath the surface that got under my own skin and made me shiver.

I kept putting up my protective psychic rose, and I'd wrap myself in white protective light before entering other people's homes, but still, I was too much my mother's daughter not to pick up psychic energy from other people. I didn't get messages or have long chats with spirits from the other side, like my mother did, but I was plenty susceptible to the unspoken energy on this side. It could be draining and exhausting.

However, a night out with Alex was a great way to try to change my focus to something positive. I enjoyed being with him. Naturally, I was drawn to his aristocratic good looks and undeniable animal magnetism. I knew he was protective of me, too. Sometimes I'd wake in the night and feel him out there. Sure enough, if I looked out my window, I might catch the shadowy form of a wolf prowling the perimeter of my garden.

Our relationship had become a lot more open when he'd admitted what I'd already guessed. That he was a werewolf. I still hadn't shared with him my own secret powers, though sometimes he looked at me with those clear, all-seeing eyes as though he sensed there was more to me than I was letting on. However, I wanted my coven's blessing before I shared my secret, and I hadn't asked them yet.

What I had given Alex, if not my full trust, was help getting his house cleaned up. Now he was working on the grounds, actually opening the formidable gates to the community for the garden competition prize-giving. I felt I could take some credit for this new Lord Fitzlupin, one who was more approachable, more open to the community. And I loved it. Not *loved him*—don't get ahead of yourselves—but more this willingness to open himself up, carve a new path. It was exactly what I'd done when I'd left the States, and then again after Jeremy died. I knew how challenging it was to reinvent oneself. I knew how wonderful it could be.

The waiter had cleared our plates by now, and Alex took my hand in his. Our fingers, so different in size and texture, interlinked. I felt safe. Around us, the other diners murmured softly. They shared food, stories about their day, perhaps tried to decide if there'd be a second date. The wide windows had been thrown open to let in a welcome summer breeze. Outside, the sun had set and soon the moon would rise, plump and nearly full.

I turned back to find Alex's intense gray-blue eyes trained on my face. They were flickering with warmth. "Something's troubling you." The encouragement to go ahead and say whatever it was that bothered me. Apart from Gillian and Greg, there was something else.

I swallowed, trying to find the right words to be discreet, but true. "With each house that I entered this week, I encountered something new about the person who owned it. Usually, something negative. With Elizabeth, I felt her loneliness. Her family is scattered and although she puts a brave face on things, I sensed how badly she missed them."

Alex nodded. "Especially with Dolores, her old friend, gone. It must be very tough."

The waiter brought my herbal tea, Alex's coffee, and our desserts. Salted dark-chocolate tart for him. Raspberry sorbet for me. Not that raspberry sorbet isn't light and refreshing, but I had terrible dessert envy. When Alex offered me a bite of his tart, I couldn't resist digging my fork in for a taste.

When I all but moaned with pleasure, Alex looked amused. "Do you want to switch?"

"No. I had a brownie this morning from Roberto's. I can't eat chocolate all the time."

I resolutely went back to my sorbet, and he wisely said nothing as he ate his tart.

My thoughts returned to the gardens I'd visited. "Vera's is wonderful, but she struggles to get around. And poor old Milton is on his last legs."

"But she has her grandson and his family now," Alex said. "They'll help her."

I agreed and spooned up some more sorbet. "And Colleen O'Brien's garden was undeniably beautiful, but there was no beauty in the way she tended it. It was almost too perfect, too well-crafted. It was missing soul. And then, of course, there's the business with her neighbors."

Alex grimaced. "Yes. I heard all about it when Colleen cornered me outside Bewitching Blooms."

I nodded. "You must have heard the venom in her voice as she spoke about Erica and Greg. Such unwavering conviction that they were out to get her and tarnish her reputation in the village by claiming she'd killed their tree. Nasty asides about them coming from London. I mean, know your audience. If she considered them outsiders, what does she think about me?"

Alex raised his eyebrows. "Not the best way to win your goodwill."

"And then the accusation that they were trying to ruin the judging by playing loud music and starting a BBQ."

Alex chuckled. "Now that I didn't know. Did they really dare?"

"Oh yes. Honestly, at first I found the whole thing amusing. Then it all turned sour when I went to the Lawleys' garden and they bickered and whined about Colleen. I wasn't kidding when I said there were bad vibes between Greg and his wife, Erica. More than just their feud with Colleen. They were really sharp with each another, quick to put one another down. It was very unpleasant."

But I wasn't telling Alex the whole truth. It was more than pettiness. There was something hard between them. And in amongst all the perfection of Colleen's garden, there was darkness lurking. I just didn't know what it was. I was going to tell him about Colleen's threat, but then I'd have to tell him about the mysteriously mobile gnomes. I wasn't going to lie to Alex, nor was I going to tell him the gnomes had magic power, so I kept that part of my troubles to myself.

I couldn't take Colleen's threats seriously. She wouldn't do harm to her neighbors over a garden competition.

Surely not.

"So when you saw Greg with Gillian, it was easy to think

the worst," Alex concluded, circling us back round to where we started.

Right. Not only were Colleen, Erica, and Greg in a nasty emotional triangle, but I was worried that there was another triangle forming. Gillian Fairfax not only drew men to her, but she had the worst taste in men of anyone I'd ever known. If she and Greg were doing more than meditating...

"It's not that I want to believe that either of them is up to no good, but there are already bad feelings between Greg and his wife. Gillian might toy with him, but she'd never go for someone so lacking in assets." That sounded harsh, but I was pretty sure it was true. "And I worry about Gillian. She can't keep making the same mistakes. It's just not safe. For her and the rest of the village. She has a bad track record around men. Let's face it."

He nodded. "At the pub, I heard her referred to as the black widow."

"Ouch. I don't want anyone else's safety in the village to be compromised. I swear, it feels like Gillian is a liability."

Alex squeezed my hand. "You can't take on everyone else's pain."

I was shocked at his astuteness, but I nodded. "All I wanted was to give out a prize for the prettiest garden. Instead, I keep falling face-first into the weeds."

We left the restaurant, and I kissed him tenderly then, inhaling the scent of his herby cologne. Even if it felt like I had the weight of the village's private lives on my shoulders, I knew I had someone good to rub them at the end of the day.

CHAPTER 14

The next day, I felt a special charge from the moment I woke up. The moon would be full tonight and our coven would gather to celebrate, to recharge and combine our energies and powers. Witches follow nature's seasons, and the cycles of the moon affect our powers. We commit ourselves to work with the earth's elements—earth, air, fire, water—and each witch has a special affinity with a particular element.

Char's (for better or worse) was fire, and I was looking forward to her focusing her energies tonight. We'd made a start together, but perhaps tonight she could draw on the strength of our sisters to harness her power and control it. She was all over the place, and I was worried she'd cause an accident. Spontaneous combustion in the farmhouse? No thanks.

I was really looking forward to seeing my sisters again. It had been a long week, spikey with the dramas of the garden competition, and I valued the warmth and open-heartedness of my coven sisters more than ever. We had such busy lives, each with our own business or workplace and family, so the full moon was often the only time everyone was present. Plus, Amanda's birthday this week made the occasion all the more special.

I spared a moment to think of Alex confined to a dungeon instead of enjoying fellowship with his kind.

It was a busy day. As anyone who's ever worked in retail or any kind of customer service can tell you, full moons bring out the crazy in all of us. There's a reason mentally ill people used to be called lunatics, as they appeared to behave more erratically during a full moon. I put up my psychic protection rose before I left the farmhouse, and I was glad I did.

Char and Norman got into the car with me and Blue.

Normie chirped, "That garden gnome's more flighty than you two."

When Char had gone to collect Yasmin, she hadn't been in the farmhouse garden. She seemed to come and go as she pleased, so I decided not to worry about it. I was certain she'd show up when she was ready.

Sure enough, when I got to Bewitching Blooms, Yasmin was perched beside the till. I didn't ask where she'd been, as it wasn't my business. No doubt she had clandestine meetings of her own. I wondered if the full moon affected gnomes. Since they were intimately connected with gardens and growing things, I suspected it did.

Imogen arrived late and frazzled, saying she'd slept in. I assured her it was fine. Everything was under control, and I sent her off to get our morning coffees from Roberto's. While she was gone, Erica Lawley came in. I was shocked by her appearance. The woman looked absolutely haggard.

She glanced wildly about, as though unsure what she was

doing in my shop. Then she saw Yasmin and physically recoiled. "Ugh, I hate those things," she cried. "They remind me of Colleen O'Brien. I've seen them peering through the fence. I'm convinced she puts them there deliberately."

Okay. My day was starting well.

"Can I help you with anything?" I asked in a soothing tone.

"Yes. You can find my husband."

"I beg your pardon?"

She put a hand into her unkempt hair. "He's disappeared. I know we haven't been getting on too well lately, but he went out yesterday and never came home. Not all night."

Did she think he'd been hiding in my shop? "I'm so sorry," I said. Naturally, my mind flipped back to the scene of Greg Lawley and Gillian Fairfax holding hands on her lawn.

"Has he done this before?" I asked.

"No. We've had arguments, and he'll go off in a huff, but he always comes back." Her voice rose as she continued. "He *always* comes back. What if something's happened to him?"

I suspected Gillian Fairfax had happened to him, but couldn't say that. I'd do some quiet digging, see if I could find out if Greg and Gillian were together.

"Surely you'd have heard if something had happened to him?"

"I don't know. Probably. I'm going out of my mind," she said. "He doesn't have many friends."

"What about work?"

"I phoned them, and he took a couple of days off. They seemed quite surprised that I didn't know anything about it."

While she was speaking, I reached for sunflowers for cheerfulness, beautifully scented jasmine for calm and good sleep, a couple of roses for love and fidelity, blue iris for hope, and added a bit of greenery. It was a casual, thrown-together bouquet, and as I wrapped the paper with string, I whispered a message of peace and calmness into the blooms. "Here," I said, handing the package to her. "Keep these near you today. They'll help."

Tears came into her eyes as she accepted the flowers. She leaned in and smelled the jasmine, and I could feel the tension ebbing from her body. "I should pay you," she said.

"No. They're a gift. Try to stay calm." I smiled. "And spend some time in your beautiful meditation garden today."

"And if he's not back by tomorrow?"

"Can you think where he might go? Does he have friends you could call?"

She shook her head. "Not really. We've always been enough for each other."

I hesitated. "If you haven't heard from him by tomorrow, you should probably call the police."

She left, clutching her bouquet, and I stood irresolute. I wasn't keen on interfering in someone else's marriage, but I also wanted to help this troubled couple if I could.

"Well, she was very rude to me," Yasmin said, sounding hurt.

Imogen returned with the coffees so we couldn't say more. When I had a quiet moment, I called Gillian and got her voicemail. I left a message asking her to call me. I debated saying it was urgent, but if I was wrong and she wasn't with Greg, I'd feel awfully foolish. I left the message at *please call me*. We weren't on the kind of terms where we chatted on the phone, so presumably she'd get that it was important.

I never heard back from Gillian all day. Other than the

niggling worry about Erica and her husband, I managed to get through the day. If a couple of customers seemed more irritable or stressed than usual, I put it down to the moon.

Still, I breathed a sigh of relief when it was time to close the shop.

Char and Norman were waiting outside. She was holding a box containing one of Roberto's famous carrot cakes. Neither of us had the time to actually bake this week, so Char suggested bringing a birthday cake—for Amanda—from her work. I thought it was the perfect addition to the potluck dinner my coven had each month.

We got in my car and headed to my mom's apartment, as it was her turn to host the full-moon festivities. She had a charming and uniquely-decorated one-bedroom flat above her occult shop on the other side of the village. Like most properties in the village, my mom's was Grade II listed, which meant it was protected as a structure of special interest, warranting every effort to preserve it. But unlike, well, anyone, my mom's interior design did nothing to nod at history.

In the back of the Range Rover, Norman was quiet. A sure sign that he was about to behave badly. I caught a glimpse of him in the rearview mirror. He was nuzzled next to Blue, who was fast asleep, of course. His bright aqua-blue feathers and lime-colored head contrasted with her stripy orange fur. He blinked his pale-yellow eyes at me.

It was the first full moon of summer. Back home in the States, the full moon in July was a Buck Moon, so-called because it was the time of year when a buck's antlers push out of their velvety foreheads and grow. It was a powerful moon, in line with the oncoming mating season when bucks would use their antlers to fight for dominance.

Mating. I was seriously worried that there might be a mating dance going on between Greg Lawley and Gillian Fairfax. And dominance. I felt that urge reflected in the competition between neighbors I'd been unhappily exposed to this week. Colleen and the couple next door weren't too dissimilar from head-locked deer. However, spiritually, a Buck Moon should be a time of embracing and manifesting new versions of yourself. Here was hoping.

I pulled up outside Mom's shop. The moon was just peeking over the hills, illuminating the leafy tops of trees and dropping its light on the world below. At its peak, I find the moon's brightness has a sound to it which rings in the sky, quietening all below it. I felt humbled, ready for the evening.

I had a key to my mom's, so I opened the door adjacent to that of the shop and led the four of us up the narrow staircase, Blue trundling behind us.

We emerged onto the landing, where we were met with the overwhelming scent of jasmine and sandalwood. Mom might have prepared for us, but her place usually smelled of some incense or other.

The door to my mom's place was ajar, and I called out a hello as we entered and went straight through to the kitchen and living room. Despite its modest size, the apartment was filled with light, some natural, the rest from multiple lamps and candles, and the overall effect was positively shining. In the eaves of the building, it had charming sloping ceilings, the original wooden beam work exposed with plenty of naturally formed nooks and crannies—perfect for my mom's eccentric collections of antiques and knick-knacks.

The living space was dominated by an open brick hearth with a log-burning fire in the middle, which, of course, was retired for the summer. But it still provided a nice focal point. In the center, she'd placed a marble statue of Luna, or Selene, the Greek goddess of the moon. A large chunk of clear quartz —for clarity of focus—sat beside her,. There was a basket of pink quartz for the sacred feminine, amethyst to help with psychic ability, not that Mom needed more of that, and moonstone to enhance the power of the moon. Large candles waited to be lit. Mom's athame, her witch's dagger, sat beside the candles along with a bowl of water which had likely been purified in moonlight.

I stood back as I watched Char take it all in.

"Wow, this place is wild," Char said, wide-eyed.

If there was one thing my mom was not afraid of, it was color. She loved jewel tones: ruby reds, rich magentas, emerald greens. The living room walls were iridescent with a gold-toned cream, but everything else was pure color. She had a fair number of potted plants, including ivy that trailed around the window. In spite of my career as a florist, Mom preferred the living plants. On the walls were pictures of our long-dead relatives, though I suspected Mom was in regular communication.

We were there to help my mom get ready and to have a visit before the others arrived.

Normie flew around, inspecting the place, then landed on the fiddle-leaf fig tree in the corner. As he wrapped his claws around a branch, he commented, "Nice perch, Cookie."

My mom's ferret, Loki, was merrily grooming himself in the corner. Loki was an albino ferret with pearly-white fur and small but watchful pink eyes. His breed meant he was prone to various health conditions, especially with his eyes and skin, so he was in and out of the vet clinic with a frequency my mom dealt with stoically. In fact, she'd cultivated such a relationship that she often dropped off gifts at the vets, small tokens of appreciation in the form of incense or homemade fudge. Playful and mysterious, Loki was the apple of my mom's eye. And he had charmed the rest of the coven, too. One of his favorite things was to entertain us with a 'weasel war' dance. Ferrets loved to dance. And if they didn't get enough play time, they'd turn to more mischievous antics, like stealing socks or shoes. We all had to keep an eye on our belongings when we gathered at Mom's.

"This place is cool," Char said, putting the cake on my mom's countertop for later.

"You can light Amanda's birthday candles with your magic," I said to Char.

Mom related her experiences in her shop today. She'd also noticed a shift in the energy of her customers, though the people who shopped in an occult and crystal shop tended to be more open to those shifts.

Char told Mom about her struggles with fire and engines.

Mom listened intently. "Well, lassie," she said when Char had finished. "You've set off on a path. It's nae an easy one, and you must take it one step at a time."

I could see Char visibly relax at Mom's words. She was trying so hard to master all her power immediately. It was good to be reminded to take things more slowly.

The witches arrived and, even though we saw each other regularly in the village, we hugged each other hello. As we shared our goodwill and energy, I felt my mood brighten. My mom buzzed around us, happy to be hosting. She was sixty-five but with the energy of a twenty-five-year-old, and her henna-red hair bounced as much as her green eyes danced. Wearing a sage-colored smock and rows of red beads, she jingled with every step.

Most of the coven were squeezed onto the two crushed-velvet sofas and adjacent embroidered poufs. Bree had chosen to sit cross-legged on the shaggy Afghan rug, and Char took a spot beside her. She was looking more and more at home in the coven.

There's no truer love than the sisterly love between witches. We all came from different walks of life, were different ages, and had different careers. What united us was our craft and embracing the magic in our lives.

I took a seat and helped myself to a plate. There was a huge array of salads and cold meats across the coffee table, and I took a little of everything. My mom had made cider, and I accepted a tall, bubbling glass.

Bree, a fabulous herbalist, was holding court with a story about her ten-year-old. "My Esther May's hay fever is bothering her something rotten," Bree was saying. "So I gave her my trusted herbs, equal parts Black Cohosh, Mullein, Poplar Bark, Coltsfoot. And then you know what that girl does? Goes with her father to Scott's farm and helped bale hay." She rolled her eyes. "I'm magic, but not even I can help runny noses and red eyes if you spend the day literally rolling around in the hay."

"That girl needs a sense spell," Lucille said, laughing her light fluttery laugh.

"My Marvin thinks you saved his life," Amanda said to Bree. To the rest of us, she explained, "My husband was bitten by a fire ant. Said the pain was intense and he couldn't bear the itching. And then these awful pus-filled pimples arrived, and he panicked. I called Bree, and she made him up a fresh aloe vera press. I don't know what else you put into it, but Marvin acted like Bree had saved him from a burning house."

Norman piped up from the corner. "No one even congratulates me when I manage a triple flip mid-air."

"Shut up, you," Char said. But she was smiling.

As usual, the gossip continued to flow, but it didn't take long before everyone turned to me to provide the juicy details of the garden competition.

"I just want to say how glad I am that none of you entered," I said with feeling.

"That bad?" Lucille laughed. She was a pre-school teacher and had a honeyed, gentle nature and was used to calming pre-teen tantrums.

If only I could soothe the tensions of our fellow Willowers with a few well-chosen words.

"There's more rivalry than I'd realized," I said. I wouldn't say more, not wanting to gossip or to bring down the mood.

Bree sensed my hesitance and turned instead to Char. "And how have your studies been going?" she asked. "Has Peony been guiding you?"

Char blushed, a rare occasion. "I've been making some progress. Peony is a big help, but I'm not quite in control yet."

Inside, I smiled. It was unlike Char to admit where she felt challenged. I could see that she longed to witness her powers grow. But she was on the right path.

After we'd visited for a while, Mom looked out the window and sure enough, the moon was at its zenith. "It's time to go," she said.

She picked up a bag she'd already packed, and we set off together.

Willow Waters is located near a river and it isn't far to walk outside of our village and reach woodland paths. They are well-traveled by dog walkers and nature lovers during the day, but tend to be deserted at night. We followed the main trail for ten minutes, then Mom led us onto a narrower path. If you didn't know it was there, you'd miss it.

We reached a clearing beside a calm pool of water. This was a magical spot.

Mom unpacked candles, and we placed them in a circle and stepped inside.

"Will you cast the circle?" Mom asked Amanda. It was an honor to be asked and no doubt she'd chosen Amanda as she'd celebrated a birthday this week.

Amanda did, then lit the candles and lifted her arms to the sky. "Spirits of the earth, air, fire, and water, we sisters gather here under the light of the full moon to seek cleansing of old wounds, old energy, and the filling up of pure, clear light. May we release the past and open ourselves to the future as we acknowledge the lunar shift and set our intentions for the month coming."

Then Amanda was silent, and we held hands, each of us letting ourselves experience this magic in our own way.

After the garden competition forced me to bear witness to the difficult dynamics of my fellow villagers, the energy of these women gripped me, renewed me. Three words buzzed around my head like a mantra. *Here. Now. Go.* Gravity pulled at my legs, and I felt like I was sinking into the moment and soon the familiar rush entered my body. I blinked through a strobe of stars and then closed my eyes. With my face raised toward the night sky, I felt the moonlight soft on my face. In that instant, a skein of brilliant color came into view beneath my eyelids. Fizzing, skittering, encompassing me in the combined strength of these women. I was here and yet I was emptied out, allowing our powers to fuse.

I felt warmth, incredible warmth. Actually, I was hot. Too hot.

I let my eyes blink open and gasped.

"Look," I whispered to Char. "Look what you did."

Within the circle, a fire was roaring. Bright flames licking against a stack of wooden logs that hadn't been there a minute ago.

Char gasped, and the chain broke.

There was a burst of laughter as my fellow witches realized what had happened. They looked at Char in amazement.

"Impressive," Amanda said.

"Very," Lucille agreed. "But you need to focus your efforts on controlling your limbic system."

"Limbic what?" Char muttered.

This was where Lucille's interest in biology, particularly the brain, became the most evident.

"The limbic system is the parts of your brain that control the primitive, reflexive states and impulses. This system is focused on the *now*. But you need to create a happy and harmonious relationship with the forebrain, or the prefrontal cortex, which is your rational decision-maker. This system can draw on a memory bank and make decisions based on the past and the future. Only with the two working together will you gain control over your powers."

Char glanced at me, stumped for a reply. Clearly, she

hadn't followed a word Lucille had said. And who could blame her?

"It's okay," I said. "It sounds more complex than it is. You just need to control your magical power. But wow, that is incredible."

Char had a dogged expression. I could tell she was having trouble taking it all in but was determined to listen. "I'm going to put the fire out," she said quietly but firmly. She closed her eyes again, and her features set in concentration. She raised both hands and then to my amazement, the words of a spell came tumbling from her mouth.

> *"Quench these flames of their roar.*
> *Cool and quell until they are no more.*
> *So I will, so mote it be*
> *So I will, so mote it be."*

And just like that, the flames went out, though the candles circling us still burned. We burst into applause. Char flushed again, pleased with herself. She was really growing up.

Suddenly the happy mood dissipated.

The candles dipped and flickered.

My mom had begun to sway and moan. Until now, I hadn't realized how quiet she'd been in our circle. But it was clear to see that someone or something had appeared to her.

"We see danger. Terrible danger. Darkness. Disguises. So much earth. Something under the surface. They are here. But they are not here."

She shook and shook.

"Mom?" I whispered, worried now, but knowing enough not to break her vision.

Her green eyes flickered open. "Oh, lassie. He's not a settled soul. He's under the earth where he shouldn't be."

Alarm skittered through me. "Who, Mom? Who is it?"

Mom shook her head. "I canna say."

CHAPTER 15

*A*n incessant buzzing juddered me awake. I blinked, stunned. Morning light crept through the crack in my bedroom curtains. I touched my temples where a tension headache throbbed. All night long, I'd been beset by terrible nightmares, and now that I was awake, a cold sensation of dread still ran through my veins. My mind still swirling, I reached around my nightstand until I found my phone.

I stared at its blinking screen. The incoming call was from my mom.

Immediately, images of her vision came flooding back to me. Darkness and earth and undiscovered danger. But as with all my mom's visions, clarity was not forthcoming. There was no face, no person, no setting. Just that disturbing vision.

After our cleansing circle in the woodlands, my coven had gone back to Mom's apartment for cake and tea, but we were subdued. We hadn't even sung happy birthday to poor Amanda.

I sat up in bed and answered Jessie Rae's call. "Mom? What is it? What's happened?"

"Oh, lassie, there you are. I thought you'd never pick up. It's terrible. I've just had a call from Erica Lawley."

"Erica?" I murmured. "You know her?" I hadn't even met the Lawleys until the garden competition.

"Yes. She and her husband buy crystals from me. And I sourced a very nice garden Buddha for them. Lovely people." My mom's tone changed again. "But Erica is frantic. Her husband is missing. She wanted to see if I could feel Greg's spirit. See where he is."

I still hadn't heard back from Gillian. What if Greg was with her?

Then I thought of Mom's vision last night. And what if he wasn't? I'd hoped the wayward husband would have returned to his wife by now.

"Don't take this the wrong way, but if this is unusual behavior for her husband, why did she call a medium, not the police?"

My mom tutted down the phone. "Och, Peony, why do you always have to be so cynical? Some people are tuned into the other realms."

"It's just not most people's first port of call, if you know what I mean." I paused, pensive. "Do you think this has something to do with your vision last night?"

"That's why I'm calling, lassie. It's not a good sign. Erica rang out of desperation. She said this was completely out of character for her husband. They have their little spats, but he always lets her know where he is. She did call the police, but they're not taking her seriously, as he isn't considered a risk to himself or to others. They advised her to wait it out today and call back if he's still not home by this evening. The poor woman really is beside herself. She's convinced that something terrible has happened."

And then my nightmares came back to me. I was lost in the woods behind the farmhouse. It was night. No full moon, no moon at all. Just darkness. I couldn't find my way out. It was as if the sky was bearing down on my chest, holding me down so I couldn't breathe. Had my mom's vision infiltrated my subconscious? Or was I picking up on some signal from elsewhere that something was sending me a message? What if Greg was in danger? He could have gone for a walk in the woods yesterday —and tripped and hit his head. Or something more sinister.

"Is his mobile ringing?" I asked.

"No, Erica says it goes straight to voicemail. I'm on my way to visit with her now. See if I can pick up anything. Do you want to come with me?"

I swallowed. This wasn't the first time my mom had tried to involve me in her psychic investigations. She believed, even though I hadn't her gift, that I helped strengthen her power.

Like I was her familiar.

"I can hear your thoughts, Peony Bellefleur. And you know as well as I that two witches are better than one. All of me hopes this is not a case of having to contact the other side...in which case, our combined powers can help figure out this chappy's whereabouts. If he's passed over, I can take over and speak with his spirit directly."

"Mom, don't you think you should let the police handle this? They're actually trained to find missing people. Besides, what if Greg's not really missing? What if he went to the pub and had a few too many?" Or something else.

"First of all, Greg doesn't even drink. It goes against his life ethos, or so Erica says. Secondly, you know that I must go where I'm led. Either you want to help, or you don't. Simple as that, lassie. But I won't be waiting 'round for you."

I could hear the worry in my mom's tone. She would consider it disrespecting her gift not to follow a cry for help like this, especially given her vision the night before.

I checked the time. A little after seven a.m. Imogen was opening the shop, and I was on the late shift. I'd looked forward to sleeping in. I sighed. "Okay, I'll meet you at Erica's house. Give me thirty minutes."

I swallowed a groan and then hung up the phone. I was torn. Part of me felt the intensity of my mom's vision last night, and a missing person the following day was not a good sign. But the other part of me suspected that if Greg was anywhere, it was Gillian's bed. I didn't care if it was early. I tried phoning Gillian again. Once more, I got her voicemail. This time I used the word *important* in my message.

Blue had been watching me this whole time, her wide eyes alert to the possibility of danger. My familiar was always there when she was needed. I stroked her soft head and was rewarded with deep purrs.

"Let's hope this is just a domestic hiccup, not something worse," I murmured.

Blue mewed in response. She didn't like the nastiness in the village, either.

"What do you think? A quick visit to Lemmington House en route to Erica's?"

Blue blinked slowly.

"I'll take that as *you love me* and *yes,*" I said.

I roused myself from bed, took a quick shower to blast

away the cobwebs, and slipped into a blue and white summer dress.

Downstairs, Char was already awake—another surprise since it was her day off from the café. By now, I knew her morning sounds. She wasn't a quiet person in the mornings. But all I could hear was the sound of the microwave and Normie flying around the hallway, his wings flapping gently. Why was Char so quiet?

"Morning, Char."

She looked up from the kitchen table, an uneaten bowl of cereal in front of her. I noted immediately those telltale blue shadows beneath her eyes. She had slept terribly.

"Bad night?" I asked, slipping into the chair next to her.

She nodded, pale and frowning. "Awful. Worst night's sleep I've ever had, and I've slept on the living room floor of rock bands."

I grimaced. There were some things, as her guardian witch (as I liked to think of myself), that I didn't need to know about Char's wayward teenage years.

"Did you have nightmares?" I asked. "I did. Terrible ones. I think Jessie Rae's vision got to us."

Char's eyes came to life. "I *did* have terrible nightmares. Not that I wish them on you, but I'm glad it wasn't just me. I dreamt about the lake. There was some kind of storm and it flooded. Water pouring everywhere. It was unstoppable. I tried and tried to make a dam with my magic, but nothing was working. I was helpless." She shook her head. "I *hate* being helpless."

As I poured coffee, I told her about Jessie Rae's phone call and seeing Gillian and Greg holding hands in Lemmington House's garden. "I'm worried." I explained that I'd promised to help my mom with Erica, but first I was going to pop in on Gillian and see if my suspicions were right. I didn't feel good speculating about Gillian, but since it might be a matter of life or death, I figured the gossip gods would forgive me. "Do you want to come with? You're off work today, right?"

Char frowned. "Wouldn't that, like, be weird?"

I shrugged. "No weirder than Erica calling a medium she barely knows to find her missing husband."

"Huh. Good point." She rubbed her eyes, then blinked a few times. The poor witch looked exhausted. She was getting her first taste of deep witch intuition. It was bound to be overwhelming.

I thought it would be a good learning opportunity for Char to put her powers to good use in the community. If Erica was as panic-stricken as my mom said, then she wouldn't bat an eyelid at a couple of hangers-on.

I downed my coffee, grabbed a banana for the road, and we were off.

To my surprise, Norman was perched on the hood of my Range Rover, waiting for us.

"Did you two dolls really think you were going on a search mission without a view from the sky?" he drawled. "I was born for this job, Cookie."

Char rolled her eyes, but I was impressed by his offer to help. "Were you eavesdropping, Normie?"

"Always on the alert, doll," he said.

"A fine quality in a familiar," I said, meaning it. "Hop in."

The three of us took off for Lemmington House. I drove a little faster than usual, aware that the longer my mom spent alone with Erica, the more mischief the two might get into. When we arrived at Lemmington House, I told Char to stay in the car, but Norman insisted on flying a lap around the grounds.

I strode up to the front door, but before I could ring the bell, someone called my name. I turned and saw Owen Jones coming toward me. He was wearing his green gardening overalls, a cap slung low on his brow to protect him from the sun.

"Morning, Peony," he said, greeting me with a nod of his head. "You're here early."

"I was hoping to catch Gillian. I tried calling, but there's no answer."

"She's away for a few days."

But I'd delivered that enormous bouquet for an important luncheon. It didn't make sense just to abandon it. Gillian lived for her little gatherings, and I knew they were few and far between for her these days.

I stared at Owen. "Was it something urgent?"

He shrugged. "She didn't say. She took an overnight bag and drove herself, if that helps."

"What if there was an emergency? Could you reach her?"

"I've got her mobile number." He must know I had it, too.

"She's not answering." Could Gillian and Greg have gone on a romantic getaway? It wasn't hard to imagine. Gillian loved the thrill of a secret tryst. I thought of Erica and my mom communing with the spirit world. How awkward if Greg was just holed up in some luxurious B&B.

Owen walked me back to the car, and he and Char did their usual overly casual greeting. It seemed to me that one of these days one of them ought to make a move. But right now I had more important matters to worry about.

If Owen had any thoughts about Gillian and Greg, he was

keeping them to himself. He said, "I'll get Gillian to call you when she gets back."

I thanked him, and Normie finally returned and swooped back inside the car.

As we pulled out, I asked him, "Everything seem normal?"

"Yup, not a rose out of place and not a person in sight. Dead or alive."

I hadn't expected anything else, but I hoped he'd have the same answer after we'd talked to Erica and Norman flew a lap around her home.

I filled him and Char in on what Owen had told me as we sped toward the Lawleys' house.

Char looked nervous as we approached the shiny red door and knocked.

"Just remember, Char, we're here to do good. It's a privilege."

She twisted her mouth, still appearing unsure, and took a deep breath as the door opened.

To my surprise, my mom was standing there. Although her expression was downcast, her eyes were shining—a sure sign that she was already deep in communion with the departed. "Thank you both for coming."

She ushered us in, then wrapped her arms around us both. "Good thinking bringing our wee one," my mom whispered. "Three witches are better than two. And two better than one. And is that Normie I spy outside?" She released us and peered through the window.

"Just in case," I said. "Where's Erica?"

"The kitchen. She's in a terrible state. I explained that you were on your way to help."

I scanned the hallway. So far nothing looked unusual about the Lawleys' house. Had I jumped to conclusions the other day, wondering why Greg had taken me around the outside to enter the garden?

We walked through to the gleaming, minimal kitchen where Erica was at the table, head in hands, long black hair hanging over her face. She glanced up as we entered. There were tears in her eyes. Erica and Greg might have had their differences, but this was a woman in real distress. Either that, or she was a fabulous actress.

I shuddered a little. I badly wanted to believe Erica was pure of heart. But I also knew the first person the police would investigate was Greg's wife. It was always those closest to a missing person who were treated with suspicion.

"Something terrible has happened to Greg. I can't bear it. And I'm certain that witch next door has something to do with it."

I felt my mom and Char bristle at the use of witch, but I decided to give Erica a free pass this time. She was worried that her husband was dead, after all. I took a seat next to her at the table. "You think Colleen knows where Greg is?"

"She's offed him!" Erica shrieked. "That woman is capable of anything."

I laid my hand on Erica's arm. "Competitive she might be, but murder? Don't you think that seems a little extreme?"

I thought Erica was overreacting. Of course, I had my suspicions about her husband's affair with Gillian to guide me, but I also couldn't imagine Colleen killing someone over a garden competition. It seemed preposterous. Their feud had gotten out of hand, and both women seemed to be losing their grip on reality.

In my most soothing tone, I told Erica that it was highly unlikely that Colleen had anything to do with Greg's disappearance. The best thing to do was to wait a couple of days and he'd turn up. Maybe he was just cooling off somewhere.

Erica shook her head, her dark hair rippling. "That's exactly what the police said. Well, I'm not having it. I can't hang around waiting to find out if my husband is dead." She appealed to my mom. "I want to contact the spirits. You said you'd help me."

I opened my mouth to object again, but Jessie Rae swooped in. "Of course, lassie," she said. She picked up a wedding photo that she must have asked Erica to dig out. She spread her arms wide and closed her eyes. "Who's with us?" she asked.

Honestly, it was as creepy as anything the first time I saw my mom do that, but after a while I got used to it.

Then Mom began to sway back and forth. In a voice nothing like her own, a deep, strangled tone, she cried, "Help me."

CHAPTER 16

*C*har and I watched helplessly as Jessie Rae stumbled into the Lawleys' garden—Greg's most sacred place, and where my mom would best be able to feel his energy. Although I knew she was for real, I was frustrated with her. No doubt she was flattered that someone in the village finally wanted to enlist her help rather than mock her talents. But it did feel like she was placating an overreaction on Erica's part. But then I recalled the terrible darkness of my mom's vision last night, followed by my own nightmares, and then Char's. Things weren't looking good for Greg.

The three of us followed. Outside, Jessie Rae's eyes were closed, and she was swaying from side to side. I noticed she was gripping something in her right hand.

I turned to Erica. "What is she holding?" I asked in a half-whisper.

Her eyes full of tears, Erica explained that it was Greg's black-jade crystal. "It was his most prized crystal. He said it helped him tap into his intuition and steer clear of negative people and situations. He thought the black jade could help him tune into the root source of negativity."

My inner alarm bells started ringing. Why was Erica using the past tense to talk about Greg? Did she know something we didn't? Was that because *she* was the cause of Greg's disappearance? Was this why she was so certain something bad had happened after her husband spent two nights away from home?

The questions kept rolling through my mind, tumbling and crashing like the waves Char had described from her dream. But I had to keep my cool. It wouldn't do to start jumping to conclusions and pointing my finger. After all, I was still pretty convinced that Greg and Gillian were cozied up at some hideaway.

Meanwhile, Jessie Rae appeared to be having a conversation with thin air. She was swaying and nodding and murmuring. Strange sounds made their way out of my mom's mouth. Not quite words, not quite grunts. She was far gone now, gone to the other side.

Erica watched on, fascinated.

"Jessie Rae hears something," my mom intoned. "The spirits. They're in turmoil. Everything churning, churning like the ocean. Waves crashing, falling. Something drops like a pin in the water but ripples and... Everything ripples."

Waves. There it was again. But what did it mean? Was my dream about being lost in the woods wrong? Had Greg drowned?

"What does it mean?" Erica whispered.

"It's not always clear," I replied. "When the spirits first appear, there are often many voices, all wanting to be heard. It's like an ocean rolling, each wave clamoring to be heard.

My mom could just be referring to that. Or it might be someone else talking through her. We have to wait."

Erica's eyes widened. I suspected she had taken on more than she had bargained for.

The tense atmosphere was interrupted by the sound of a car squealing along the street and coming to a sudden stop outside the house.

Erica jumped back. "I'd know that sound anywhere. It's Daddy's Rolls Royce. I knew he'd come." She rushed out of the side gate. She'd forgotten all about my mom, who was still swaying and murmuring under her breath.

Jessie Rae opened her eyes, sensing a shift in the atmosphere, and then swiftly closed them again. The spirits were still calling her, and it was her duty to listen.

A moment later, Erica returned with two people who I assumed were her parents. Her father was a tall, silver-haired, dapper-looking man, dressed in a crisp linen suit, a heavy gold watch glinting at his wrist. Behind him was a petite woman, smaller even than Erica, with a nervous expression. She wore a blue and white floral summer dress, as did I, but there the similarity ended. Hers looked like a crisply-ironed designer creation. There was something diminutive even about her walk, and I could easily see how this large burly man dominated both women in his family.

"Thank you for coming," Erica was saying. "I've been beside myself. I didn't know what to do."

The mother patted her daughter's hair, and the father said, "I'm here now. Daddy will sort it all out. He always does. Tell me everything that's happened since we spoke."

Wow. He spoke about himself in the third person.

Neither parent had acknowledged the other people in

their daughter's garden. And I didn't think it was going to help anyone to have the domineering Daddy around if and when the husband came back from his philandering. Talk about awkward.

Erica said, "A constable came and asked me questions. He took away a photo of Greg and said to call if I heard from him. He asked about places Greg likes to visit, friends. That sort of thing."

"Good. And what's being done? Is there a nationwide search underway?"

Erica looked miserable. "No. The police said they'd look for him. And warned me that since he's more than eighteen, if he's found and doesn't want me to know where he is, they can't tell me."

"What?" the man thundered the word. "Do they suspect he left you voluntarily? What nonsense."

"I told the constable I suspect foul play. That evil woman next door is behind Greg's disappearance. I know it!" Erica sobbed.

"All right, dear. All right," her mother soothed.

Suddenly, Jessie Rae broke from her trance. Just in time. I couldn't imagine her powers going down well with Erica's stern father.

I tried to catch her eye, but her gaze was trained on a spot near the fence. Did she sense where the tree had been cut down? It had been a living thing, after all. I never knew what my mom was going to pick up on.

Daddy cut off his wife's question to their daughter about when she'd last seen Greg, by saying, "Who are these people?"

Jessie Rae stepped toward him. She looked pale. "I'm a

medium," she explained, entirely unabashed in front of the unimpressed Daddy. "And I sense death nearby."

Daddy's silver eyebrows shot up, and his wife let out a tiny sound.

"Now you look here," he said. "I will not have you frightening my daughter. How much is she paying you?" he demanded.

"I offer my gift freely," my mom replied with dignity. Then she shuddered. "*Violent* death," she moaned and stumbled toward the fence. If there was one thing you could say about Jessie Rae, it was that she was truly fearless.

Daddy stared at her, aghast. Probably, he wasn't used to dealing with a medium in the throes of a vision.

Erica, probably guessing that her father didn't believe her neighbor had murdered her husband, told her parents about the murder of the tree. And about all the nasty things Colleen had done and said. Erica nearly ran out of breath before she concluded, "And then she threatened me and Greg."

"What?" That got Daddy's attention. And everyone else's except Jessie Rae's.

"Our neighbor accused us of sabotaging her chances of winning the local garden competition and said she'd make us sorry."

I didn't want to add fuel to the fire, but I felt I ought to mention that Colleen had said something similar to me in my shop.

Daddy listened, and I felt him weighing the evidence, very much the judge. Then he said, "It warrants further investigation."

"But the police said—"

"You leave the police to me. I've got connections in high

places. It's time Greg Lawley's disappearance was taken seriously."

~

To my horror, I realized that Jessie Rae was leading me and Char to Colleen O'Brien's garden. Now this was a lady who would not take three women and a parrot, who suddenly swooped down to join us, wandering onto her property lightly. "Mom? This is so not a good idea. Colleen has quite a temper, and she's *very* protective about her garden."

"There's a spirit in the garden who's calling to Jessie Rae," she intoned. "They want to be heard. They *need* to be heard." Okay, my mom spoke about herself in third person too, but it was different somehow. She didn't do it to be pompous.

"I've been surveying Erica's place, but now I'll take a look around Colleen's," Norman told us, obviously excited by the drama. "See if she's home. And warn you if she is. How about three 'macaws' if there's danger?" He didn't wait for an answer, but flapped his wings and off he soared.

"He's there. We can feel him, poor restless spirit," my mom said.

I sighed. I knew the strength of Jessie Rae's powers, but this seemed like a step too far, even for her. In a hush, I said, "Come on, think about it. Would Colleen O'Brien really murder her neighbor over a gardening competition? It's crazy."

Finally, my mom turned to face me. With unshakeable conviction she said, "You know as well as I, lassie, that many a death has happened for frivolous reasons."

Hmm. She had me there.

And now we were entering Colleen's garden. Trespassing. Were we breaking the law? I was already dreaming up my excuse when the homeowner confronted me, as I was certain she would. The best I could come up with was that I'd wanted another look at her garden for judging purposes. And Jessie Rae and Char were my...assistants?

"Wow," Char said as we emerged from the side alley into Colleen's garden. "This place is like a page from a posh gardening magazine." Then she gasped and pointed.

To our amazement, Colleen's gnomes had arranged them-selves in a circle around the fountain with the stone angel statue.

"What the—?" Char gasped again.

"The gnomes are trying to tell us something," I said. Not a sentence I ever thought I'd utter.

I glanced around the garden nervously, half expecting Colleen to emerge from the kitchen brandishing a bread knife. But maybe she hadn't noticed us. Yet.

Jessie Rae closed her eyes again and began to sway. "Oh, we feel it. The spirit is lying here. And they are angry. There's so much anger. Oh, our vision is filled with red. A wall of terrible color. A wall. So heavy. I feel the weight."

I went to the fountain and crouched beside the gnomes, expecting one of them to explain their position. But this bunch was not as forthcoming as my Yasmin. "What are you trying to tell us?" I asked. "Has something bad happened on this site?"

I waited. Nothing. Not a peep.

The gnomes did not move an inch. Their perfect circle of six smiling faces reminded me a bit of our coven meeting. They sported hoes and spades, the flute of course, and there was a milkmaid. The only thing that made them strange was the way they were standing. I could not imagine that Colleen had arranged them like this.

And that's when I noticed the ground they were standing on. The area had been graveled over, but in front of the gnome with the spade was a bare patch of dirt as though he'd begun digging and given up. I looked closer. Not so much as a weed grew. It was as though the soil was dead.

I pushed the gravel away in a different area and it was the same. Unlike the rest of the garden, nothing grew on the patch beneath the angel. It was barren. Dry.

"How strange," I murmured.

And then I remembered what Arthur Higginsbottom had told me at the gardening committee. I'd only been half listening, but he'd said the early Roman conquerors had salted the earth as part of a custom purifying or consecrating a destroyed city. The process cursed anyone who dared to rebuild the site. Nothing would grow where the earth was salted.

Out loud, I paraphrased Arthur's words, *"Burying things under the earth doesn't get rid of them. Just hides them, sometimes for hundreds of years."*

"What's that?" Char asked. "Part of some spell?"

I shook my head and then stood up straight. "Char, can you search for something on your phone?"

She nodded and pulled out her phone, which was newer than mine. Her fingers hovered over the screen.

"How much salt does a human body contain?" I asked.

Char's fingers froze. She glanced up at me, then at the ground. She took a step back. And tapped at her phone. She continued typing and then squinted at the screen. She cleared her throat. "*Sodium facilitates many bodily functions, including fluid volume and acid-base balance. An adult human body contains about 250 grams of salt.*"

"Hmm, 250 grams?" Jessie Rae murmured. "Och, that's a lot."

Again, I recalled Arthur's words. *Of course, the soil around here isn't actually salty per se. Otherwise we wouldn't have so many lovely gardens.*

I knew that flowers hated salty earth. Most—except for the salt-tolerant ones that grew along beaches and roadsides —simply refused to grow. I looked back at the dead ground around the fountain, then the gnomes' unblinking faces, then up at the angel. If only I could ask him what he knew.

Char came closer. She, too, stared at the ground and then at the angel. "Oh, Angel Gabriel," she said. "If only you could talk."

"Wait, what? Did you say Angel Gabriel?"

"Well, he's blowing a horn, isn't he? We had lots of pictures of Archangel Gabriel in the convent. That's usually Gabriel blowing the horn. He was the messenger of God who told Mary she'd be with child." Char turned toward the alley, clearly wanting to leave. "Can we go now? I don't like being here."

Neither did I.

I caught a flash of movement in a window in Colleen's house and glanced up to see a face disappear. Colleen must have seen us and chosen to stay inside.

Because she had something to hide?

CHAPTER 17

*J*essie Rae was a firm believer in many things: the afterlife, elves, iridology, and the power of demolishing a good buttercream-topped cupcake once a week, but the police were not one of them. She was suspicious of all officers, all detectives, and far preferred to solve any mystery with the aid of a spirit from the afterlife than a living, breathing law enforcer.

So as you might well imagine, the three of us stood outside Colleen's at an impasse.

"Peony," my mom said, drawing out my name. I knew immediately that I was in trouble, because she rarely used my birth-given name. "I'm just saying we've got this far without help. Why don't we find Colleen ourselves and get her to answer our questions? It's the obvious way forward."

I sighed. Why didn't my mom listen? "Because *if* we're right, there's big trouble lurking beneath that fountain and angel statue. If Erica's right, Colleen murdered Greg and buried him beneath the fountain. And so confronting

Colleen would be dangerous. And stupid. And did I mention dangerous?"

Char piped up, "I vote we go get spades. Dig up the ground. See for ourselves. I can do most of it. I've got the muscles." She rolled back the sleeve of her T-shirt and flexed her biceps. She was definitely the fittest of the three of us.

I tried again. "Erica's father said he'll call his high-up connections in law enforcement. Why don't we let them handle it?" Both Char and Jessie Rae looked mutinous, so I said, "Are you going to start digging up that woman's garden now? In broad daylight? If you do, the police will come, all right. To arrest you two."

"I'd have thought my own daughter would have more gumption," Mom said, sounding offended. "Very well, then. We'll come back after dark."

So not what I was going for, but at least I had a reprieve. I'd think of something to prevent the two of them from coming back tonight. I had a few hours to come up with something.

As I was about to get into my Range Rover, the chatty mailman came along, whistling. "Morning," Marty said, flashing some envelopes before putting them in the Lawleys' mailbox. "Some ashram is writing to them from India. I've heard about people going there on silent retreats." He shook his head. "My wife tells me I should go on a silent retreat. It's a joke because she says I can't stay silent for five minutes."

I said good morning, wisely didn't comment on Marty's chattiness, and I—along with Jessie Rae, Char, and Norman —piled into the car. And I set off for the high street. After the morning's excitement, we fell quiet. No doubt they were both working out how they'd dig up Colleen O'Brien's garden without waking her tonight. A terrible idea that I'd be trying to talk them out of.

I trusted my mom's instincts, and I trusted mine. I trusted the power of three witches to uncover a buried mystery. But to murder someone over a garden competition? Even if there was a deep prior disagreement, it was a long stretch. Downright crazy, even. But as Mom said, people did violent things in the heat of the moment. Things they might come to regret for the rest of their lives. Was Colleen O'Brien one of these people? Was Greg Lawley her unfortunate victim?

I dropped my mom at her shop, then took Char and Norman to the farmhouse. Char opened the car door and slipped out, but I called her back for a moment.

"Char, something happened to you in Colleen's garden."

She looked pensive for a moment and then admitted, "The statue of Gabriel above the fountain," she said. "He was crying. At first, they looked like real tears. I swear, they were tumbling down his face. But then I figured the water feature had malfunctioned and made the statue look way weirder than it was. Still, I have a terrible feeling about Colleen O'Brien. A garden *that* perfect is the brainchild of a control freak. Believe me, I met a few of those at the convent. I know what I'm talking about." She paused and shuddered. "When you're that tightly wound, it doesn't take much for the whole thing to unravel and cause chaos." She closed the car door with a flourish.

Colleen O'Brien was definitely tightly wound, but had her fury at her neighbors resulted in murder?

∼

Back at Bewitching Blooms, Imogen had had another busy morning. Alongside our usual weekly deliveries, a huge order had come through for a surprise birthday party. The customer, a proud husband and new dad, wanted to fill their entire home with white roses as a special gift to his wife, who had given birth to their first child. It was going to be difficult to source as many roses as he'd requested, but I wasn't complaining. The business was good, and I had to get my head back in the florist game.

Imogen and I worked steadily, wordlessly communicating and helping each other to get on top of orders and the mountain of paperwork, which defied my attempts to slim it down. Imogen seemed lost in her own thoughts, and I was grateful. Normally, she loved to hear village gossip, but I couldn't talk about what had happened today. For now, any suspicions I had about Colleen, and worry over Greg's whereabouts, would belong to me and me only. I wanted to protect Erica from any rumors which might begin to fly around the village. She was upset enough.

As disturbing as it had been seeing those gnomes in a ring around that barren ground, I still half believed Greg would simply walk back through his front door, kiss his wife hello, and ask what was for dinner. Or better still, bring dinner home with him. And maybe some flowers, too, to say sorry for disappearing without telling his wife where he had gone. But with my mom's vision, the dead earth around Colleen's fountain, and Char's vision of a crying statue, and also her dream and mine too, I wasn't full of confidence that everything would turn out right.

Erica's father might not be my idea of a great dad, but he definitely looked like someone who got things done. If he said he was going to investigate Colleen O'Brien's property, I was fairly certain he would.

I felt like none of this would ever have happened if I hadn't agreed to judge the Willow Waters Prettiest Garden Competition.

Why hadn't I listened to the people who'd warned me it wouldn't be all sunshine and roses?

CHAPTER 18

The next morning, the garden competition committee was due to meet at the rectory for another breakfast meeting to fuel us for visiting the six finalists' gardens. Exactly the last thing on earth I felt like doing. The competition had been way, *way* more than I'd bargained for, and now my thoughts were full of subterfuge and murder —not gardens full of pretty flowers. But since I couldn't shirk my duties, and I needed to talk to Justine without Arthur and Bernard hearing, I drove to the rectory early, still dozy from yet another bad night's sleep.

Justine opened the rectory door with a warm smile and ushered me in. I'd texted her to let her know I was coming early and in her deep plummy voice, she told me that she had a pot of strong coffee brewing. The smell alone revived me, and I knew immediately I'd made the right decision in turning to Justine for help.

I followed her through to the kitchen and took a seat at the table. She had already laid out an array of pastries. Obviously, I didn't need asking twice before tucking into a pain au chocolat.

Justine grabbed a couple of mugs from the drying rack and then sat across from me.

"Tell me," she said, matter-of-factly, "what's been going on? Have the contestants been overwhelming you with gifts? Like homemade jam? Or coming in droves to your shop and purchasing your most expensive bouquets? Are you being hounded?" She chuckled, a throaty, warm sound which instantly filled me with calm.

"Ha. If only." I took a sip of coffee. "It's a little more sinister than that. I thought you might be able to help. Confidentially."

"You're in the right place. The Lord and I take people's secrets very seriously."

I took a deep breath and explained that the feud between Colleen O'Brien and the Lawleys had gone far beyond the issue of the dead tree. The two households were quite literally at each other's throats. Now, and worst of all, Greg was missing—even if his status as a missing person had yet to be confirmed by the police. Colleen was a clear suspect, although of course we still had to abide by the rule of innocent until proven guilty. I kept the gnomes' strange behavior, my mom's vision of an unsettled soul under the earth, and Char's vision of a crying statue out of my confession.

Still, these were startling revelations and Justine was understandably shocked. "But surely Erica Lawley doesn't truly believe her neighbor did away with her husband for a winning certificate printed off the church computer and a certificate to a gardening center?"

When she put it like that, the theory did sound preposterous.

"I'm suggesting that Colleen O'Brien should be disqualified, that's all."

"Even if Greg turns up safe and sound, which I'm sure he will, Colleen has not conducted herself in a manner which befits the community values of the competition. The way she spoke about her neighbors is..." Justine paused and shook her head so vehemently her brown bob bounced from side to side. "Still, do we need to make a public declaration? Or might we simply make sure she doesn't receive a prize?"

"The latter is probably best." Just hearing Justine's sensible take on it all made me realize my instincts were right. "Do you think Arthur and Bernard will agree? They rhapsodized about Colleen's previous entries, remember? And she's the darling of the Willow Waters Prettiest Garden Competition. *The Willow Waters Weekly* had a double spread on her winning irises last year. I saw it in her memory book."

"They'll have to listen. The truth speaks for itself, I find." She picked a croissant from the spread and tore a corner.

Arthur Higginsbottom arrived then, looking excited at the prospect of a day out judging gardens. He was dressed formally and a little haphazardly, as usual, and his eyes shone with excitement. "We've six lovely gardens to visit today. I can tell you now, ladies, that we won't always agree. Sometimes discussion can get quite heated, but it all works out in the end."

When Bernard arrived, we all sat at the table with coffee and pastries and Bernard showed us a computer printout. He'd mapped out the most efficient route to visit all six gardens without backtracking.

"Before we begin, we need to address some nastiness which has sadly arisen in the competition," Justine said.

Arthur snapped up his head, surprised. "Nastiness? What nastiness? Historically—if you forgive my little penchant for history—this has always been a very *friendly* competition."

Hmm. Pull the other one. Willowers were wildly competitive. I was just the only one not to realize it until now.

"I'm afraid so," I said. "As you know, a feud between Colleen O'Brien and her neighbors, the Lawleys, has been brewing for some time. But it seems the competition has escalated matters somewhat."

Justine cleared her throat. "Colleen has come to both Peony and to me with quite wild accusations about sabotage, pointing the finger at Erica and Greg Lawley and refusing to back down. And the Lawleys have accused Colleen of wrong-doing as well."

"But the Lawleys didn't make the finals," Bernard said, clearly confused.

"No, but they believe Colleen O'Brien killed off their tree when they were on holiday. And there are other accusations against Colleen," Justine said. "We believe she should not be allowed to win."

"Whatever do you mean?" Bernard asked. "Colleen worships her garden, and it's historically the best. It's what she lives for."

Sadly, I was worried it was this very fact which had derailed Colleen's sense of decency.

Arthur's forehead crinkled, and he shook his head. "I know Colleen has something of a temper on her, but this seems a stretch."

"Frankly, Peony and I think Colleen should be disqualified from the competition as a result of her behavior."

The men gasped.

"Disqualified?" Bernard echoed. He'd remained completely silent while Justine and I spoke. I recalled the warmth and admiration in his voice at our last meeting as he described Colleen's prize-winning irises. His expression now was crestfallen.

I felt terrible, like I was the one causing all the trouble in the village.

"She's crossed the line," Justine said firmly.

Arthur took my clipboard page of notes and thumbed through the pages. Then he swiped through the photographs I'd taken on my phone and sent to him and the other judges. His face lit up, and I knew he was impressed. As he might well be. Colleen was an expert gardener. But that couldn't excuse her behavior.

"Her garden is exquisite," he said. "It does seem an awful shame to disqualify her over some bad blood between neighbors." He returned his gaze to the photographs. "Her garden is so perfect."

I glanced at Bernard as he poured milk into his coffee and the two colors swirled together.

Finally, Bernard lifted his head. "I say we trust the vicar and Peony on this one. If they say Colleen's behavior breaks the rules, then it does. It's our community values and the spirit of togetherness which holds this competition together. It's not the Chelsea Flower Show." He smiled a little sadly. "As much as I wish it was. But we won't publicly shame Colleen. That'd be against our community values as well. We'll just agree that she won't win a prize this year. That will be punishment enough."

We all agreed, fortunately, and then agreed that we'd still visit her garden and make a show of judging it so our absence wouldn't feed the rumor mill.

"Right," Bernard said. "If you've all finished your coffee and pastries, let's get started. To the Tewksburys."

"The Tewksburys," Justine agreed.

They'd been shortlisted from Arthur's list. Liza Tewksbury owned the greengrocer on the high street. Her shop had been in the family for generations and she ran the business with her husband, Don, who came from a family of farmers. Arthur had said their garden was wonderful. Modern, bold, daring. I was looking forward to this visit. From there, we'd visit Vera Brown and then Colleen O'Brien. I couldn't wait to get that visit over with. I wished I could find an excuse not to go.

We all piled into my Range Rover, and Bernard gave me directions to the Tewksburys' home—using his computer printout with the most efficient route to visit the finalists.

While I drove, I couldn't keep my mind on the competition. The more time passed, the more I became worried about Greg's whereabouts. Mom had texted me earlier to say he was still missing, and I'd called Gillian again, once more getting her voicemail. I was beginning to loathe the sound of her message, all snooty and implying she'd call you back if she didn't have something more interesting to do.

We four judges dutifully surveyed the Tewksburys' garden, which was incredible. Bold and modern, just as Arthur said. I didn't like it as much as Vera's, but it was impressive all the same.

When we got to Vera's garden, it was as beautiful as I remembered. Milton ambled over to greet all of us and wagged his tail when I slipped him a liver treat.

Then we headed to Colleen's. When we arrived, I saw two squad cars in the street. My heart picked up speed. Could there be news of some kind about Greg?

If the others noticed, they showed the kind of British restraint where you don't mention it if you see police cars near your neighbor's house. I followed suit and pretended I didn't see them either as I parked my Range Rover.

We knocked on Colleen's door and she opened it. She was wearing all green, as though to remind us she was from the Emerald Isle. She faltered when she saw me standing with the other judges, then treated us all to a broad smile. "I'm looking forward to showing you what I've done this year," she said to Arthur. "I think you'll be pleased." Then she led us to her kitchen and through the alley to her garden.

I noticed that the gnomes had all been put back where they belonged, and they'd stayed put. At least for now.

The garden was an oasis of perfection. The fountain gave out the soothing sound of water bubbling. Every flower seemed to have bloomed especially to impress us all. The peace and beauty almost made me doubt what I'd seen only a day earlier.

Almost.

While Colleen pointed out the highlights of her garden to the two men, Justine said, "I think that was your doorbell, Colleen."

"Oh, I wonder who it could be." She excused herself and the next thing we heard was shouting.

We all looked at each other.

CHAPTER 19

"*Maybe* I can help," Justine said, racing through the kitchen door.

I followed her and heard a certain Scottish-accented voice. What on earth was my mother doing here?

When I reached the front hall, it was quite the scene. A man in a suit identified himself as DCI Hutchinson. With him were four uniformed constables, two carrying shovels. Behind them were Erica's father, Erica, and Jessie Rae. I doubted this was standard operating procedure, but Erica's father seemed like the kind of man who made the extraordinary happen.

"I've a warrant to search your home and garden, Mrs. O'Brien," said DCI Hutchinson, handing her a piece of official-looking paper.

"It's an outrage." Colleen stomped her foot. "I won't stand for it."

Justine and I stood back as Colleen unleashed more of her venom.

With a nod from the DCI, the constables pushed past

Colleen and entered her home. Two went upstairs while the other two headed toward the back of the ground floor. Jessie Rae followed them in but stopped beside me. Colleen stood, watching, fury etched on her face.

"There you are, lassie," my mom said. "I've been asked to guide the police. We'll be bringing comfort to this restless spirit soon enough. I can feel the earth turning beneath our feet." My mom said these words so confidently that I gazed in wonder.

Maybe these officers were open-minded. Or maybe Erica's father was using any excuse to search Colleen's home and garden, even if he didn't trust my mom as the source.

Meanwhile, Colleen was trying to block the alley to her garden. "This is an outrage," she screeched. "Preposterous. I've never been so insulted in all my life. Why, if my husband was here, this would never happen. But he's in Ireland, doing the work of a saint, and now you're taking advantage of a lonely, vulnerable old woman."

"Would you like me to escort you to the station for a cup of tea while my officers do their work?" the DCI asked Colleen.

"No, I would not," she replied roughly.

She ran into her garden, and we all followed. "You be careful on my lawns and with my flowers. This garden is a precious, prize-worthy place, and you'll be sorry if you do it any harm." Then she shrieked. "What do you think you're doing with those spades?"

Bernard and Arthur appeared stunned. As well they might.

"Perhaps we should move on to the next garden," Arthur said, looking embarrassed.

"No," Colleen cried. "I want witnesses to this police brutality to a helpless woman who's all alone."

Jessie Rae said to DCI Hutchinson, "There. Under the fountain. That's where the poor man lies."

"What poor man?" Bernard asked.

"This way," Jessie Rae said confidently. My mom was not fazed by the drama. She'd seen much worse from the spirits whose restlessness tended to make them tetchy. She led the two constables with shovels to the fountain.

Erica's dad, dressed in another smart, expensive-looking suit far too warm for the summer weather, stayed close to his daughter. Whatever conversations had taken place in my absence, he had also decided to treat my mother cordially. "What did the Bellefleur woman say?"

"He's under the fountain," Erica replied in a small voice.

He repeated her words to the DCI and the officers, and they nodded in return. They were under his thumb, and I wondered how he'd done it.

Colleen ran to the fountain and stood in front of it. "How can you desecrate my garden? And have you no respect for the angels?" Her Irish accent grew broader the more angry she became.

The moment the officers stuck their shovels in the ground, Colleen began to wail. I'm talking banshee levels. Piteous, funereal sounds. I half expected her to beat her chest and tear out chunks of her hair.

"You won't get away with this," she cried. "I'll see to that. This is an infringement of my human rights." She ran to Arthur, Bernard, and Justine, who were huddled together in shock. "Can't you stop them? You're the vicar and leading members of the community. They'll listen to you."

I went to Arthur and said, "You see where the ground's dead under the gravel. We think Greg Lawley could be under there."

He blinked in astonishment. "Greg Lawley? Under that fountain?"

"Yes. I got the idea from you, talking about how they used to sow the ground with salt in ancient history. The human body contains 250 grams of salt, you see."

Arthur's expression turned appalled. "But it could be anything under there. Maybe they laid their pets to rest in that spot."

I hadn't thought of that.

He took a step in the direction of the two officers, who were really putting their backs into digging. Possibly because the big boss was watching.

Arthur said, "Anyway, Greg Lawley couldn't be under there. The soil would be freshly dug."

CHAPTER 20

"*P*eony," Arthur said, "I think you've made a dreadful mistake."

I was torn between horrified embarrassment and dread. How had I let my mother and my suspicions get us all into this hideous situation?

What would happen if they found an old pet dog buried under that fountain? Could they arrest Jessie Rae and me for some crime? Malicious mischief maybe?

And yet I knew my mom wasn't a fake. And Char had seen the angel statue cry. We'd all witnessed the gnomes standing in an accusing circle. But then, gnomes had a mischievous side, as I'd discovered.

I didn't know what to do.

I felt terrible for Erica, witnessing her terror as she watched the digging. I could see the stream of anxious thoughts crossing her face. I went to her, took her hand and squeezed. It felt like holding a tiny, frail bird.

The two officers were strong. Their efforts showed in the sweat running down their faces as they dug into the ground around the fountain. You couldn't hear the water splashing now. We heard the clink of shovel against gravel and underneath the rocks in soil, along with the heavy breathing of the constables digging.

Colleen was still wailing—a warbling, constant sound, like a metronome dropped on a stone floor. By now, her anger had been replaced by woe. "My garden," she sobbed. "My precious garden."

"My husband!" Erica cried back. "What have you done with him?"

Her father put an arm around her shoulder. His face was tense, but his expression was flat, smooth as a sea-worn pebble. I couldn't tell if he thought this little escapade would prove him right (my mom was a fraud) and reassure his daughter, or if he was holding himself steady, preparing for the worst. His wife was nowhere in sight.

Next to me, Jessie Rae began to tremble. She closed her eyes. "Oh, the spirits are angry. We see righteous fury."

Erica's dad shot daggers in our direction. Erica let out another sob. The sound ripped through me.

The constables continued to dig.

Suddenly, I became aware of a new presence. A prickling came over my body. I turned, and there he was.

"Alex!" I said, "What are you doing here?" I was so happy to see him. The full moon was over, and it was safe now for him to be out in public, and I longed to throw myself into his arms but restrained myself.

"I was going by and saw your Range Rover. And the police cars. I wanted to make sure you were all right and see if you needed any help."

He glanced at Colleen, who'd yet to notice his arrival. "By

the looks of it, my instincts were right." His teeth were slightly bared, and his usually sparkling eyes had narrowed to suspicious slits. It wasn't the first time Alex's canine nature had revealed itself outside of the full moon. Small changes came over his body when he experienced anger or felt protective.

Alex turned his piercing eyes to me, and I held his gaze. "There's something beneath the fountain. Can you feel it, too?"

"No." But he lifted his head and sniffed the air. "Something doesn't smell right, though. I smell...decay."

Both of the constables abruptly stopped digging and leaned closer to the ground.

Colleen froze.

Erica cried.

My mom moaned and swayed and moaned some more.

Alex and I stepped forward.

One of the constables turned to DCI Hutchinson. "Sir, you'd better come and look."

Erica cried out, "Bones. It's bones!"

CHAPTER 21

*E*rica's dad was the first to react. "Are they human?"

"My Greg!" Erica shrieked. She'd have rushed toward the digging, but her father held her back. She turned and screamed at Colleen, "You killed him!"

"I did nothing of the sort," Colleen retorted. "What nonsense. It's probably a previous owner's pet. And now you've ruined my beautiful garden." Her mouth was grim, her forehead pinched. It was chilling, how quickly she had calmed down. Her wailing and whining were all but a memory. How was she playing it so cool? Unless the bones truly were a pet's.

I strode to the fountain. Buried in the dry soil was a bone, all right, and it was connected to another bone.

"That's not a dog," Alex said beside me.

"Greg," Erica sobbed, collapsing against her father.

"Darling!" a voice cried out from behind us. "What's going on?"

In unison, Erica, the police, Colleen, my mom, Alex, and I spun toward the alley beside Colleen's house.

And there stood Greg. A very much alive-and-kicking Greg. A tanned, relaxed-looking Greg. He stared back at us with bemusement.

"Are you Greg Lawley?" DCI Hutchinson asked, sounding bemused.

"I am. What's going on here?" he asked again. "I saw the police cars and heard the commotion."

Erica screamed and collapsed against her dad.

He held his daughter's limp body, aghast. "I think she's fainted," he said.

Greg ran to his wife and cupped her face in his hands. He murmured into her ear, stroking back her long hair, which had fallen across her cheeks. Her eyes fluttered open.

"Erica, it's all right. I'm here."

"You're alive," she whispered.

"Of course, I'm alive. I was only at a silent meditation retreat, not white-water rafting in Chile."

"What?" Erica straightened and smoothed down her dress. "What do you mean?"

"You knew where I was. I left you a note. I signed up for that silent meditation retreat in Bedlam Bottom in Hampshire. I showed you the flyer."

"Retreat?" Erica repeated, her eyes widening. "Retreat?"

Now I remembered the flyer that Marty, the postman, had delivered. Greg had left it on the garden table during my judging visit, and Erica had tried to throw it away. The action led to a little spat about Greg's search for enlightenment.

"UNPLUG," Greg explained. "Remember? We digitally detoxed, so my phone was switched off. I left you a note on your bedside table."

"I never saw a note. Why did you leave it there? You know

I have piles of books beside the bed. How on earth was I supposed to find it? You should have told me you were going, not left me a note. I've been worried sick. I thought you were dead."

"Good Lord," Erica's father said, glaring daggers at Greg. "All this fuss and you were off 'ohmming' somewhere?"

"I thought she'd murdered you!" Erica said. "Have you any idea what I've been through these last few days? I lost my mind."

"That's right!" Colleen yelled. "You owe me an apology and compensation for what you've done to my beautiful garden. Now I want you all to leave. I'm calling my solicitor."

"Well, I've already called mine," Erica's father shot back.

Jessie Rae flitted over to the fence to try to meditate, the two constables rested on their spades, catching their breath, and DCI Hutchinson was on his phone—while the neighbors did what they did best. Argued.

What the Lawleys and Colleen seemed to have forgotten was that there was still a body in Colleen's garden.

Who was in the hole? Alex and I returned our attention to the bones.

And then it dawned on me. All the pieces of the puzzle came together in one clear vision. Of course. Part of me had known it all along. I just needed the evidence.

"You know," Alex said quietly. "Don't you?"

I nodded, my mouth grim, and stepped forward.

In a firm voice, I said, "These bones belong to Gabriel O'Brien."

At that, everyone stopped talking.

Colleen blinked at me furiously. "What on earth are you on about?" she barked.

"The body in the hole belongs to your husband. That's why you placed the statue of the angel Gabriel on top of the fountain. In some twisted commemoration. And that's why nothing grows in this patch of earth. I noticed on my first visit that the ground here was dry and barren. At the committee meeting, Arthur told me early Roman conquerors salted the earth as part of a custom purifying or consecrating a destroyed city. It cursed anyone who dared to rebuild it. But salt also stops flowers from growing. An adult human contains about 250 grams of salt. I put the two things together."

"Don't be so stupid," she said to me. "There are all kinds of nutrients in a human body that would encourage flowers to grow, and the salt would wash away with the rain."

Greg stepped forward and stared at her. "Not if you threw a lot of garden lime into the hole to degrade the body faster." He glanced at me. "I remember seeing her unloading big bags of the stuff and wondering why anyone would need so much garden lime. If she put too much in the hole, hoping to speed up the decay, that would scorch the plant roots and kill them." He glared at his neighbor. "The lime probably leached into our garden, too, and helped kill our tree."

Colleen began to wail again. This time, the sound took on a sharper, truer note.

"Is she right, Colleen?" Arthur asked. Arthur, who knew all about old secrets buried underground, went to Colleen. "You'll feel better if you get it off your chest. I'm sure your husband's death was an accident."

Colleen grabbed onto him as though he were a life raft and she was going under. "That's it. You're right. It was an accident. I never meant to harm him. My lovely Gabriel.

Everything was fine for the first thirty-eight years we were married. He'd go to work. I had my garden. He'd help me on the weekends and his holidays. And then..."

I held my breath, waiting for her to continue.

She shook her head, her expression turning furious. "And then he retired. That's when it all went wrong. He interfered in everything I did, from cooking to the garden. Every time I turned around, he was there, watching over my shoulder, breathing down my neck. It made my skin crawl." She shuddered. "I told him to find a hobby of his own. I made so many good suggestions. Golfing or a book club. I even proposed the local history society, Arthur. Gabriel would have enjoyed that."

"He would have," Arthur agreed.

"But would he listen to me? No. 'I enjoy being home with you,' he'd say. But I didn't like it. As soon as he didn't have coworkers to manage, he tried managing me. When he told me he was going to uproot the Irish shamrocks and move them to a better spot, I lost my mind and hit him over the head with my shovel." Her shoulders sank.

My shoulders sank as well.

"Like I would a rat I caught threatening my garden. Didn't even think. Just swung the shovel. He fell down, and I thought he might have a concussion. I got a cold cloth for his head. Rubbed his hands. Begged him to wake up." She sniffed and wiped her eyes.

I could see the scene playing out and I felt nausea rise.

"But he didn't. He wouldn't wake up."

"I'm so sorry," Arthur said, and I could tell he really was. He and Colleen were old friends, after all.

She kept talking to him, and the rest of us stayed silent. It was as though only the two of them were in the garden.

"I never meant to hurt him. You know I wouldn't do that deliberately. I loved him."

Arthur nodded. "I know."

"I didn't know what to do. So I buried Gabriel here in the garden. It's what he would have wanted. Hard work it was, too, and I'm not as young as I was. But I got him underground nice and tidy. And, yes, I threw in a load of garden lime to make it all nice and tidy. Then I bought this very expensive fountain and stone angel, so he had a proper grave marker. I laid him to rest with his namesake. The angel Gabriel."

"Did you use the same shovel to bury him that you killed him with, Colleen?" I asked, unimpressed.

"You've no right to judge me," she spat. "When you've lived with the same person for forty years, see how you feel."

"But you kept everyone thinking he was alive, talking about how he was caring for his ailing mother in Ireland. How he'd be back at Christmas. And then you went one step further, sending postcards and parcels from Ireland. I saw a postcard being delivered just the other day. You did it to keep everyone from questioning his sudden disappearance. And his pension checks kept arriving."

"Well, what was I supposed to live on?"

The police had heard it all, of course. They listened as Colleen confessed her terrible deed and waited until she had explained herself before approaching her.

"Colleen O'Brien," DCI Hutchinson said. "I am arresting you for the murder of Gabriel O'Brien." As the detective read her rights, she dropped her head and began to cry.

The rest of us remained in her garden, stunned. The two constables who'd been upstairs returned and led her away.

DCI Hutchinson gave orders for the two remaining constables to guard the site until the forensics team arrived.

Greg and Erica were clutching each other.

"I'm sorry," Greg kept saying. "So sorry you were worried."

"I'm sorry, too. I should have been more understanding."

"How did you know?" Erica's father asked my mom. He looked stunned, all his cool, calm suavity vanished in the face of a medium's true power.

"The spirits, dearie. Never underestimate the power of the spirit world. They commune with us all the time, and we must be open to their truths."

"How did *you* know it was Gabriel under there?" Alex asked me quietly, taking my hands in his.

"I think I've been putting the pieces together slowly over the past week. I noticed the small things, and later they wove together to tell a story. The mail Marty was delivering around the village, the dry earth by Colleen's fountain, Arthur's story about salt. If only I had remembered about Greg's silent retreat flyer, I could have saved Erica a ton of worry."

Alex squeezed my hands. "But then we might never have discovered poor Gabriel O'Brien. He was a good man. I'll always remember him with a smile on his face and a cheerful greeting. You would have liked him. And now he can be laid to rest. Properly."

We both glanced back at the hole. Poor Gabriel.

I looked around at Colleen's perfect garden. It was astounding what darkness could lie beneath such beauty.

CHAPTER 22

*B*y the time the prize-giving ceremony for the Willow Waters Prettiest Garden Competition rolled 'round, talk of Gabriel's murder and Colleen O'Brien's arrest had rippled through the village and begun to recede. Still, everyone was talking about it. Some were surprised that after all those years of marriage, she would murder her husband. Those who'd been in the village longer cited countless instances of her temper and irritability and had no problem imagining Colleen as a killer.

But her confession spoke for itself and once forensics confirmed that the bones did indeed belong to Gabriel O'Brien, Colleen remained in custody, charged with the murder of her husband.

She'd had him buried under that fountain for more than a year, collecting his pension checks and dropping him into conversation every now and again to keep up the charade. Just thinking about it made me shiver.

Greg and Erica, now reunited, barely noticed that they hadn't made the garden competition finals. Strangely, they had become the village's sweetheart couple, receiving much sympathy for putting up with Colleen, the neighbor from hell. Even though they'd been no angels themselves. They thanked my mom and me profusely for our help putting Colleen away, which my mom lapped up, of course. It wasn't often that her special gift was praised in the village. Tolerated, more like.

For my part, I was happy that Gabriel's spirit could finally be put to rest and Willow Waters was freed from another dangerous individual.

Arthur had taken it upon himself to visit Colleen in jail and reported that she was holding up as well as could be expected. Justine also visited, more from professional duty, I suspected, than desire. Even though Colleen was Catholic, Justine chose to visit her.

As for Gillian, she returned to the village a day after Greg. There had been a moment where I'd thought those two had been at the silent meditation retreat together. I mean, stranger things have happened in Willow Waters. And Gillian *had* expressed an interest in meditation.

As it turned out, she'd been invited on a last-minute trip to Cannes and dropped her commitments to jet off to the Riviera. She didn't say who her companion was, which was kind of suspicious. If Gillian had ditched important lunch guests, who'd been worthy of a one hundred fifty quid bouquet ordered specifically to match a new silk dress, I was fairly certain she'd gone to Cannes with a man. Probably an unsuitable one. Gillian returned, glowing and golden, completely unaware that I had suspected her of having (another) ill-advised affair.

I don't mind admitting that I felt pretty guilty for jumping to conclusions about Gillian again. Okay, so it was true that usually my hunches about her poor romantic decisions were right. But from now on, I vowed to give her the benefit of the doubt. Just because Greg was helping Gillian learn some meditation techniques didn't mean she was showing off her other techniques, if you get what I mean. It was just a shame Gillian wasn't warmer to the women in the village. She could do with some allies.

But back to the gardening competition.

As you know, Alex had volunteered to host the prize-giving ceremony. It was an enormous shock to everyone, considering how few people had ever seen his remote castle up close, let alone crossed the threshold. Rumors had long abounded of ghosts and hauntings, towers that weren't far from crumbling, and an ancient torture chamber in the dungeon. To be fair to Alex, he'd done a great job of maintaining his reputation as a reclusive bachelor, but despite our efforts to keep things on the down-low, word had got out that we were dating. And now suddenly he was opening up his grounds to anyone who wanted to attend the gardening competition ceremony. Lots of people, I knew, wouldn't be able to resist the opportunity to wander around Alex's gardens, even if the castle itself was still out of bounds.

I was happy to see so many of my fellow villagers at Fitzlupin Castle when I arrived clutching the bouquet I'd conceded to make for second prize. I'd argued that it was a strange prize for people who had beautiful gardens, but Arthur reminded me that it was all about the photo opp. I wasn't sure if he was right or not, but once more my wares would appear in the local paper, so I made a really pretty bouquet.

Fitzlupin Castle had been in the Stanford family for hundreds of years and it was an architectural highlight of Willow Waters. Set back from the country lanes by way of a no-through road, the estate comprised a house, tower, and extensive outbuildings, including stables. All surrounded by that now-dry medieval moat.

People milled around the grounds, taking their time to observe each detail before making their way to the garden. I'd driven with my mom, Char, and Hilary, and they were as awed by getting an invite to the castle as the rest of the villagers.

In the days which followed Colleen's arrest, Justine, Arthur, Bernard, and I had still managed to visit the rest of the shortlisted gardens as a group, then called one final meeting to decide who would win and the order of the runners-up. I'll admit, once the drama was over, it was pretty fun visiting the other gardens and debating their various merits. I was filled with ideas about how to improve my farmhouse garden, and I welcomed the new mood of optimism after a week of darkness.

Alex, too, had obviously been inspired by the village's joint effort to get their gardens looking their best. A lot of work had gone into his grounds, and I noted the addition of the impressive topiary in the driveway and flanking the main entrance to the castle.

But it wasn't until I turned the corner and clapped eyes on the sprawling back gardens that I really appreciated the transformation. Whoever had helped Alex had done a stunning job.

The heritage stone walls had been cleaned, and the beds had been landscaped with naturalistic planting, the shapes echoing the sweeping curves of the circular castle. Flower and plant choices were colorful and lively, but there were also pockets of quiet, contemplative space. The fruit orchard had been weeded and tidied. And within the dry moat, tall ornamental grasses and white geranium sprang up. They swayed and rustled in the light breeze, catching the constantly changing light. The lawns were neatly mown, dotted with garden tables and chairs with bright white parasols to shade the villagers from the summer sun.

Alex had rented enough garden furniture and dishes, glasses, and cutlery for the whole village. He'd given his own small staff the day off, and it was caterers who manned the food table and wandered around with trays of champagne, orange juice, and sparkling water, as well as canapés.

The crowd was even larger than I expected, milling around happily, experiencing the softening of the castle landscape. A huge trestle table had been set up at one end, manned by attentive waitstaff in white shirts who refilled glasses and served food. It was another aspect of the day which Alex had generously funded. A small stage had been erected and rows of white garden chairs were laid out for the ceremony.

It was all very official. I swallowed, suddenly nervous. It was my job to announce second prize and present my bouquet.

I spotted George, Alex's butler, and his wife, Annabel. It was the first time I'd seen George not wearing his formal uniform. Not to say that he wasn't looking smart in a very dapper beige suit, starched white shirt, and brown brogues polished to a high shine. Annabel was on his arm in a floral blue summer dress, her frizz of white hair pulled up into a high bun. Her rosy cheeks shone, and she smiled and gazed at the crowd with obvious pleasure.

I went to them and said how nice it was to see them both again.

"It's just like the old days," George said happily.

I recalled how he'd told me that Alex's ancestors used to throw grand balls in the enormous drawing room, which sometimes lasted entire weekends. He'd regaled me with stories of champagne-fueled lunches and lavish dinners.

"We feel that Alexander is coming back to public life," Annabel said. "And that has a lot to do with you, my dear, if you don't mind me saying so."

I didn't, but still, I had to correct her. "He's a man who knows his own mind."

"He's a man who's stronger with a woman by his side," Annabel said, her eyes twinkling.

Thankfully, I was saved from the awkward moment by the man himself.

"You look beautiful," Alex said, looking relaxed and at ease even with all these people in his garden.

I couldn't help but smile. I was happy I'd bothered with my appearance more than usual, wearing a yellow linen sundress and taking time to do my make-up and hair.

"It's amazing. The garden is quite transformed. How did you do it?" I asked.

Alex glanced past me. "I might have had a little help from a friend." I followed his gaze across the neat lawns to where Owen Jones was talking to Char. My mom and Hilary chatted beside them.

I raised my brows. "I think Owen might be the hardest-working gardener in all of Willow Waters. Where does he find the time?"

"He's a night owl," Alex said, a cryptic expression on his face. "Very happy to work into the wee hours." He gestured at the prize bouquet in my arms. "I'll get that put in some water for you."

I passed over the blooms gratefully. Of course, I'd imbued them with a quick spell of consolation (for second place) and pride for hard work.

Just then, Arthur Higginsbottom called Alex away, no doubt to help encourage everyone to take their places.

I started to search for the other judges, but someone placed a hand on my back. I turned and saw *The Willow Waters Weekly* editor and reporter, Darcie Crane.

She grinned at me, her hazel eyes shining behind her clear square glasses. "Peony," she said. "I'm hoping to interview you later."

I assumed she wanted my thoughts on the garden competition, but she said, "We always get scooped on hard news, but I thought I'd do a feature on you and what it was like to be right there when the police dug up Gabriel O'Brien."

Talking to the press about a murder was the last thing I wanted to do. I shuddered. "I don't even want to think about that day, never mind relive it." I glanced at my mother. If anyone would revel in publicity, it would be her. "You should talk to Jessie Rae," I said. "She was there as well."

"Okay. But if you change your mind, please call me."

I took Darcie's card and tucked it away, knowing I wouldn't be calling. This village was full of nosy people. I didn't want any more attention than I could help.

Darcie didn't move. She said, "I thought working for *The*

Willow Waters Weekly would be dull, but there's so much drama in this village. I've always wanted to do investigative journalism. Go deep undercover, you know. Protecting my sources and all that. Now it's coming true. Really big-name reporters have been calling me for background on the sensational Garden Statue Murder, as they've taken to calling it." She gestured at the stage where Felix was circulating, trying out different angles. "And Felix was the first photographer on the scene. Every time they use his photos, he gets credited. He's pretty excited about that."

Darcie excused herself, and I saw why.

Erica and Greg Lawley had arrived, holding hands. Together, they emanated a calm I hadn't witnessed before. Maybe it was the silent meditation retreat working its wonders, but I suspected the prospect of losing one another had reminded them of what made them fall in love in the first place. I wished them well.

The crowd began to take their seats. It was finally time for me to take my position on stage and help announce the three winners of this year's Willow Waters Prettiest Garden Competition.

CHAPTER 23

I climbed the steps to the stage where Justine, Bernard, and Arthur were waiting for me. My beautiful bouquet was elegantly displayed in one of Alex's cut-crystal vases. Arthur was flushed with excitement. He'd prepared a speech about the history of gardens in Willow Waters, and Justine was ready to add her piece about community morale.

I took my seat as Arthur went to the podium and launched into his speech. Looking out across the crowd, it was so nice to see so many familiar faces. It was comforting to see the whole community in one place. There were my coven sisters: Char, Jessie Rae, Bree, Lucille, and Amanda. The women of the WI, led by Elizabeth Sanderson. Dr. Harlan, head GP at the local private health clinic, sat with Gillian Fairfax. Vera, with Milton snoozing at her feet, sipped tea alongside her grandson and his family. I saw these familiar faces but also people I didn't know.

The competition was every bit as popular as everyone had told me.

When Arthur finished his speech, Justine took the stand. "We are very proud of what our gardeners have managed to achieve this summer. Large or small, mature or new, each garden is beautiful, each one with its own unique look and atmosphere. It was amazing to see the passion and energy and sheer effort you have all put into your gardens. In fact, you've given me plenty of ideas and inspiration for my own! I can confidently speak on behalf of all of my fellow judges when I say it's been a real pleasure to visit your gardens, and thank you to our entrants for the warm welcome. And all the biscuits. The many, many biscuits."

The crowd chuckled.

"Of course, with so many impressive gardens, it was a tough job for us judges to choose the top three. It was my and Peony's first year as judges, and you put us through our paces."

Another laugh from the crowd. This one was slightly more nervous.

"Once a shortlist was established, all judges visited the lucky few before retiring to the rectory to battle it out over tea and scones. Our three winners could not be more different from one another, but one thing we all agreed on was that these gardens impressed us with their dedication and creativity. So much so, that we've made an addition to reward our gardeners' innovation."

She paused. The crowd waited. I could feel the pressure of their bated breath.

"The winners are as follows... In third place, with their incredible stonework, is the Strong family."

They had been on Bernard's list and had designed an amazing rockery made from the local stone. Applause sounded, and Bernard stepped forward to give the Strongs their stack of gardening books. Arthur shook their hands and gave them the official gardening competition certificate.

"In second place, with their inventive take on the English country garden, are Liza and Don Tewksbury."

More applause, and I presented them with their bouquet, though they sensibly decided to leave it in water until they were ready to go. I shook their hands, and Arthur presented them with their certificate.

Justine cleared her throat. "Before we announce the winner, it's time for our authentically innovative garden prize. This was a new category added especially for this year's competition."

A stunned hush came over the crowd. No one was expecting a fourth prize.

Justine allowed for another dramatic pause. And then there was furious clapping as she announced Erica and Greg Lawley's meditation garden. "Their garden wowed the judges with its innovation and commitment to authenticity. We found it a calm and wonderful place to visit."

Okay, it was strange to give them a prize when they hadn't made the finals, but there was nothing normal about this year's competition and from the enthusiastic response, it was clear that the audience was as thrilled as the Lawleys.

Erica and Greg, flushed with happiness, came onto the stage and accepted their certificate. I could only imagine Colleen O'Brien rolling in fury inside her prison cell.

When the applause died down, Justine readied herself for the grand prize. "The garden which takes first prize and stole our hearts is a classic. Romantic, quintessentially English, its nods to native Cotswolds flowers and its sumptuous pastel color palette and array of roses made it a veritable master-piece of variety." She glanced around. "Can I say how pleased we all are to announce that the winner of this year's Willow Waters Prettiest Garden Competition is Vera Brown?"

Vera turned to Neil, who helped her out of her seat. Milton raised his head and then put it down again. The applause was as thunderous as applause can be, delivered outside on a warm July day.

I grinned, pleased with our joint decision. When each of us had visited Vera's rose garden, we'd been immersed in a peaceful tranquility none of the other gardens had managed —not even Erica and Greg's zen garden. Vera's mature age made the feat even more impressive. She must have labored for hours and hours, and her natural flair for planting and colors shone brightly.

Neil accompanied his grandmother on stage, and she leaned on him for support up the few steps. But once on stage, Vera's steps were as light as a young girl's. She happily posed with the vicar as she accepted the gift voucher for the garden center and her certificate. Felix snapped away, and Vera's smile was radiant.

It brought me enormous pleasure to see her so happy, and the same sentiment emanated from the crowd. It was the perfect way to end a tumultuous and difficult competition.

With the ceremony over, the crowd left their seats and returned to the food and drinks table, refreshing their plates and glasses and enjoying the glorious summer sun. A quartet played in the background, and the villagers went back to mingling. This had to be the true essence of an English garden party.

From my position on the stage, I watched people congratulating the winners. I spotted Gillian talking with the Lawleys, and Vera chatting with Elizabeth Sanderson. And then my gaze locked with Alex's. He endowed me with one of the most beautiful and genuine smiles I've ever seen—before walking over to the stage. He waited at the bottom of the stairs, arm outstretched, and I took his hand as I allowed him to guide me down.

"All in all, I think that went pretty well," Alex said, eyes twinkling. "Don't you think?"

"Well, we encouraged the village to keep their gardens pretty and solved a murder no one knew had been committed. So, all in all, I'd agree."

He didn't let go of my hand as he led me toward the food table. I went willingly, thinking how much I loved this village. It was peaceful, picturesque, and home to some truly lovely gardens and people.

Okay, sometimes bad things happened here. I really hoped the murder of Gabriel O'Brien would mark the end of the recent drama in Willow Waters. Maybe now things would go back to normal.

I saw Felix gathering the winners for a photo in front of one of Alex's newly planted flower beds. I was about to glance away when I caught a flash of yellow. And there was Yasmin, in the background of the photo, looking for all the world as though she'd always been there, her watering can poised over a clump of daisies.

Suddenly I had a sneaking suspicion that things in Willow Waters were never going to be normal.

But then Alex handed me a glass of champagne and said, "Come on. I want to show you my favorite part of my garden. It's hidden away from prying eyes."

That sounded good to me.

~

Thanks for reading *Luck of the Iris*. I hope you'll consider leaving a review, it really helps.

While you're waiting for the next *Village Flower Shop* adventure, have you tried my *The Great Witches Baking Show* series yet? Here's a peek from book 1.

~

The Great Witches Baking Show, Prologue

ELSPETH PEACH COULD NOT HAVE CONJURED A MORE beautiful day. Broomewode Hall glowed in the spring sunshine. The golden Cotswolds stone manor house was a Georgian masterpiece, and its symmetrical windows winked at her as though it knew her secrets and promised to keep them. Green lawns stretched their arms wide, and an ornamental lake seemed to welcome the swans floating serene and elegant on its surface.

But if she shifted her gaze just an inch to the left, the sense of peace and tranquility broke into a million pieces. Trucks and trailers had invaded the grounds, large tents were already in place, and she could see electricians and carpenters and painters at work on the twelve cooking stations. As the star judge of the wildly popular TV series *The Great British Baking Contest,* Elspeth Peach liked to cast her discerning eye over the setup to make sure that everything was perfect.

When the reality show became a hit, Elspeth Peach had been rocketed to a household name. She'd have been just as happy to be left alone in relative obscurity, writing cookbooks and devising new recipes. When she'd first agreed to judge amateur bakers, she'd imagined a tiny production watched only by serious foodies, and with a limited run. Had she known the show would become an international success, she never would have agreed to become so public a figure. Because Elspeth Peach had an important secret to keep. She was an excellent baker, but she was an even better witch.

Elspeth had made a foolish mistake. Baking made her happy, and she wanted to spread some of that joy to others. But she never envisaged how popular the series would become or how closely she'd be scrutinized by The British Witches Council, the governing body of witches in the UK. The council wielded great power, and any witch who didn't follow the rules was punished.

When she'd been unknown, she'd been able to fudge the borders of rule-following a bit. She always obeyed the main tenet of a white witch—do no harm. However, she wasn't so good at the dictates about not interfering with mortals without good reason. Now, she knew she was being watched very carefully, and she'd have to be vigilant. Still, as nervous as she was about her own position, she was more worried about her brand-new co-host.

Jonathon Pine was another famous British baker. His cookbooks rivaled hers in popularity and sales, so it shouldn't have been a surprise that he'd been chosen as her co-judge. Except that Jonathon was also a witch.

She'd argued passionately against the council's decision

to have him as her co-judge, but it was no good. She was stuck with him. And that put the only cloud in the blue sky of this lovely day.

To her surprise, she saw Jonathon approaching her. She'd imagined he'd be the type to turn up a minute before cameras began rolling. He was an attractive man of about fifty with sparkling blue eyes and thick, dark hair. However, at this moment he looked sheepish, more like a sulky boy than a baking celebrity. Her innate empathy led her to get right to the issue that was obviously bothering him, and since she was at least twenty years his senior, she said in a motherly tone, "Has somebody been a naughty witch?"

He met her gaze then. "You know I have. I'm sorry, Elspeth. The council says I have to do this show." He poked at a stone with the toe of his signature cowboy boot—one of his affectations, along with the blue shirts he always wore to bring out the color of his admittedly very pretty eyes.

"But how are you going to manage it?"

"I'm hoping you'll help me."

She shook her head at him. "Five best-selling books and a consultant to how many bakeries and restaurants? What were you thinking?"

He jutted out his bottom lip. "It started as a bit of a lark, but things got out of control. I became addicted to the fame."

"But you know we're not allowed to use our magic for personal gain."

He'd dug out the stone now with the toe of his boot, and his attention dropped to the divot he'd made in the lawn. "I know, I know. It all started innocently enough. This woman I met said no man can bake a proper scone. Well, I decided to show her that wasn't true by baking her the best scone she'd ever tasted. All right, I used a spell, since I couldn't bake a scone or anything else, for that matter. But it was a matter of principle. And then one thing led to another."

"Tell me the truth, Jonathon. Can you bake at all? Without using magic, I mean."

A worm crawled lazily across the exposed dirt, and he followed its path. She found herself watching the slow, curling brown body too, hoping. Finally, he admitted, "I can't boil water."

She could see that the council had come up with the perfect punishment for him by making the man who couldn't bake a celebrity judge. He was going to be publicly humiliated. But, unfortunately, so was she.

He groaned. "If only I'd said no to that first book deal. That's when the real trouble started."

Privately, she thought it was when he magicked a scone into being. It was too easy to become addicted to praise and far too easy to slip into inappropriate uses of magic. One bad move could snowball into catastrophe. And now look where they were.

When he raised his blue eyes to meet hers, he looked quite desperate. "The council told me I had to learn how to bake and come and do this show without using any magic at all." He sighed. "Or else."

"Or else?" Her eyes squinted as though the sun were blinding her, but really she dreaded the answer.

He lowered his voice. "Banishment."

She took a sharp breath. "As bad as that?"

He nodded. "And you're not entirely innocent either, you

know. They told me you've been handing out your magic like it's warm milk and cuddles. You've got to stop, Elspeth, or it's banishment for you, too."

She swallowed. Her heart pounded. She couldn't believe the council had sent her a message via Jonathon rather than calling her in themselves. She'd never used her magic for personal gain, as Jonathon had. She simply couldn't bear to see these poor, helpless amateur bakers blunder when she could help. They were so sweet and eager. She became attached to them all. So sometimes she turned on an oven if a baker forgot or saved the biscuits from burning, the custard from curdling. She'd thought no one had noticed.

However, she had steel in her as well as warm milk, and she spoke quite sternly to her new co-host. "Then we must make absolutely certain that nothing goes wrong this season. You will practice every recipe before the show. Learn what makes a good crumpet, loaf of bread and Victoria sponge. You will study harder than you ever have in your life, Jonathon. I will help you where I can, but I won't go down with you."

He leveled her with an equally steely gaze. "All right. And you won't interfere. If some show contestant forgets to turn their oven on, you don't make it happen by magic."

Oh dear. So they *did* know all about her little intervention in Season Two.

"And if somebody's caramelized sugar starts to burn, you do not save it."

Oh dear. And that.

"Fine. I will let them flail and fail, poor dears."

"And I'll learn enough to get by. We'll manage, Elspeth."

The word banishment floated in the air between them like the soft breeze.

"We'll have to."

Read the rest of *The Great Witches Baking Show* or sign up for my newsletter at NancyWarrenAuthor.com to hear about all of my new releases.

A Note from Nancy

Dear Reader,

Thank you for reading *Luck of the Iris*. I hope you'll consider leaving a review and please tell your friends who like flowers and paranormal cozy mysteries. Review on Amazon, Goodreads or BookBub.

I'm always grateful for the help and support of friends and readers. *Luck of the Iris* is a title dreamed up by the brilliant Linda J. Hall. Linda loves a good pun and my life would be infinitely poorer without her in it. Thanks, Linda. I think you'll see a few more of your titles coming up in this series. Thanks to all my beta readers who catch my mistakes before the books are published. A special thanks to Andy Jackson in this book for saving me from myself, plot wise.

Join my newsletter for a free prequel, *Tangles and Treasons*, the exciting tale of how the gorgeous Rafe Crosyer, from *The Vampire Knitting Club* series, was turned into a vampire.

I hope to see you in my private Facebook Group. It's a lot of fun. www.facebook.com/groups/NancyWarrenKnitwits

Until next time,
Happy Reading,

Nancy

ALSO BY NANCY WARREN

The best way to keep up with new releases, plus enjoy bonus content and prizes is to join Nancy's newsletter at NancyWarrenAuthor.com or join her in her private Facebook group Nancy Warren's Knitwits.

Village Flower Shop: Paranormal Cozy Mystery

In a picture-perfect Cotswold village, flowers, witches, and murder make quite the bouquet for flower shop owner Peony Bellefleur.

Peony Dreadful - Book 1

Karma Camellia - Book 2

Highway to Hellebore - Book 3

Luck of the Iris - Book 4

Vampire Knitting Club: Paranormal Cozy Mystery

Lucy Swift inherits an Oxford knitting shop and the late-night knitting club vampires who live downstairs.

Tangles and Treasons - a free prequel for Nancy's newsletter subscribers

The Vampire Knitting Club - Book 1

Stitches and Witches - Book 2

Crochet and Cauldrons - Book 3

Stockings and Spells - Book 4

Purls and Potions - Book 5

Fair Isle and Fortunes - Book 6

Lace and Lies - Book 7

Bobbles and Broomsticks - Book 8

Popcorn and Poltergeists - Book 9

Garters and Gargoyles - Book 10

Diamonds and Daggers - Book 11

Herringbones and Hexes - Book 12

Ribbing and Runes - Book 13

Mosaics and Magic - Book 14

Cat's Paws and Curses - A Holiday Whodunnit

Vampire Knitting Club Boxed Set: Books 1-3

Vampire Knitting Club Boxed Set: Books 4-6

Vampire Knitting Club Boxed Set: Books 7-9

Vampire Knitting Club Boxed Set: Books 10-12

Vampire Knitting Club: Cornwall: Paranormal Cozy Mystery

Boston-bred witch Jennifer Cunningham agrees to run a knitting and yarn shop in a fishing village in Cornwall, England—with characters from the Oxford-set *Vampire Knitting Club* series.

The Vampire Knitting Club: Cornwall - Book 1

Vampire Book Club: Paranormal Women's Fiction Cozy Mystery

Seattle witch Quinn Callahan's midlife crisis is interrupted when she gets sent to Ballydehag, Ireland, to run an unusual bookshop.

Crossing the Lines - Prequel

The Vampire Book Club - Book 1

Chapter and Curse - Book 2

A Spelling Mistake - Book 3

A Poisonous Review - Book 4

Great Witches Baking Show: Paranormal Culinary Cozy Mystery

Poppy Wilkinson, an American with English roots, joins a reality show to win the crown of Britain's Best Baker—and to get inside Broomewode Hall to uncover the secrets of her past.

The Great Witches Baking Show - Book 1

Baker's Coven - Book 2

A Rolling Scone - Book 3

A Bundt Instrument - Book 4

Blood, Sweat and Tiers - Book 5

Crumbs and Misdemeanors - Book 6

A Cream of Passion - Book 7

Cakes and Pains - Book 8

Whisk and Reward - Book 9

Gingerdead House - A Holiday Whodunnit

The Great Witches Baking Show Boxed Set: Books 1-3

The Great Witches Baking Show Boxed Set: Books 4-6 (includes bonus novella)

The Great Witches Baking Show Boxed Set: Books 7-9

Toni Diamond Mysteries

Toni Diamond is a successful saleswoman for Lady Bianca Cosmetics in this series of humorous cozy mysteries.

Frosted Shadow - Book 1

Ultimate Concealer - Book 2

Midnight Shimmer - Book 3

A Diamond Choker For Christmas - A Holiday Whodunnit

Toni Diamond Mysteries Boxed Set: Books 1-4

The Almost Wives Club: Contemporary Romantic Comedy

An enchanted wedding dress is a matchmaker in this series of romantic comedies where five runaway brides find out who the best men really are.

The Almost Wives Club: Kate - Book 1

Secondhand Bride - Book 2

Bridesmaid for Hire - Book 3

The Wedding Flight - Book 4

If the Dress Fits - Book 5

The Almost Wives Club Boxed Set: Books 1-5

Take a Chance: Contemporary Romance

Meet the Chance family, a cobbled together family of eleven kids who are all grown up and finding their ways in life and love.

Chance Encounter - Prequel

Kiss a Girl in the Rain - Book 1

Iris in Bloom - Book 2

Blueprint for a Kiss - Book 3

Every Rose - Book 4

Love to Go - Book 5

The Sheriff's Sweet Surrender - Book 6

The Daisy Game - Book 7

Take a Chance Boxed Set: Prequel and Books 1-3

Abigail Dixon Mysteries: 1920s Cozy Historical Mystery

In 1920s Paris everything is très chic, except murder.

Death of a Flapper - Book 1

For a complete list of books, check out Nancy's website at
NancyWarrenAuthor.com

ABOUT THE AUTHOR

Nancy Warren is the USA Today Bestselling author of more than 100 novels. She's originally from Vancouver, Canada, though she tends to wander and has lived in England, Italy, and California at various times. While living in Oxford she dreamed up The Vampire Knitting Club. Favorite moments include being the answer to a crossword puzzle clue in Canada's National Post newspaper, being featured on the front page of the New York Times when her book *Speed Dating* launched Harlequin's NASCAR series, and being nominated three times for Romance Writers of America's RITA award. She has an MA in Creative Writing from Bath Spa University. She's an avid hiker, loves chocolate, and most of all, loves to hear from readers!

The best way to stay in touch is to sign up for Nancy's newsletter at NancyWarrenAuthor.com or www.facebook.com/groups/NancyWarrenKnitwits

To learn more about Nancy and her books
NancyWarrenAuthor.com

facebook.com/AuthorNancyWarren

twitter.com/nancywarren1

instagram.com/nancywarrenauthor

amazon.com/Nancy-Warren/e/B001H6NM5Q

goodreads.com/nancywarren

bookbub.com/authors/nancy-warren